FOR BLOOD MONEY

A Bitten Twice Novel

FOR

BLOOD

MONEY

BOOK THREE IN THE MACEDO INK SERIES

BY

BITTEN TWICE

FOR BLOOD MONEY

A Bitten Twice Novel

FOR BLOOD MONEY: Copyright © 2011 by Bitten Twice

PRINT ISBN: 978-0-9839569-3-8

PUBLISHED BY: Hylton Publishing, LLC

GRAPHIC DESIGN BY: Olivia Terrizzi

Acknowledgements

Thank you to everyone who helped me create this novel. I won't call out names and bore everyone with a long list. Well perhaps a quick general shout out won't hurt.

Thank you to my friends and family, I know this one was hard on all of you as it pressed to come out. I'm paying attention now, I promise.

Thank you for the readers who continue to read and explore the Macedo Ink Series. I appreciate you adding the book to your TBR shelves.

For everyone who inspires me to keep writing.

Love

B

CONTENTS

PREFACE

The ride over the mountains had been just as grueling on the body as the last battle. Alexander twisted in his saddle raising his hand to halt his following troops. His eyes roved over his dust clad weary troops. A smile played at the corner of his lips, as his men tried to straighten their aching backs at his glance. A distant thundering returned his attention to the winding path ahead of him. One hand gravitated to the hilt of his sword, while the other shielded his eyes from the last gleaming rays of the setting sun. He could feel the breezes toying with the three plumes in his helmet; the wind was in his favor. He watched Black Cleitus, an officer in his Macedonian army, spring forward to greet the approaching scout.

The two horses pranced at the meeting, one sucking exorbitant amounts of air from the long run then exhaling mists into the chill afternoon air. Moments passed before Black Cleitus turned his horse on his heels and cantered back to Alexander.

"What word have you?" Alexander queried, eyeing the young scout beyond Black Cleitus, who seemed to have less breath than his mount.

"The King of Phrygia sends message that he would be honored if you would consider wintering in Gordium." Black Cleitus responded.

Alexander sighed squinting at his dirt-ridden pale-faced friend, for Black Cleitus was a military title, rather than one that considered his skin.

"What say you? The men and horses are weary and could use the rest, sire." Black Cleitus prompted.

"So be it; we will make good of the offer and rest well before journeying onwards." Alexander nodded.

Black Cleitus turned nodding to the waiting scout off in the distance, who wheeled about and raced back down the mountain.

Alexander stared at the town nestled in the foothills, taking account of the temples and most prominent edifices.

"Black Cleitus, I see they worship Zeus."

"I'm seeing the same, sire," Black Cleitus mumbled.

"What is that object by the temple?" Alexander leaned forward in his saddle staring at the front of the temple that sat high in the hills.

"In truth, Sire, it appears to be a cart of sorts." Black Cleitus mumbled again.

"Why would they abandon such a plain object in front of Zeus' temple? There must be something behind it, some story, some something? I cannot believe they would worship Zeus with a cart that appears to be so uncared for." Alexander furrowed his brows in frustration, waving his hands as he spoke. Once in a while he would catch a glimpse of Black Cleitus' patient face.

"I'm not sure, Sire, but I'll be sure to ask."

"Be sure you do Cleitus. My curiosity on that matter desires to be sated." Alexander's mind wandered to his conquests. He was entering Gordium as an undefeated King, but something was missing for him. He could feel the muscles of Bucephalus bunch with each proud footstep. A good run would clear his mind, but they had already traveled far and he had asked much of both his horse and his men. Alexander sighed, content with his thoughts. The remainder of the ride was quiet until they reached Gordium.

Mumbles of exhausted relief traveled like distant thunder.

The infantry made camp outside the city while Alexander, Black Cleitus and his Royal guard rode on through the city of Gordium at the request of the King of Phrygia.

He came to a halt in front of a rotund balding man, whose head was topped with a crown of leaves. He had been sitting on the front steps of an architectural mass that Alexander presumed to be the palace.

"Well, you must be King Alexander," the man's voice boomed.

"Indeed," Alexander smiled, "and you would be?"

"I would be the King of Phrygia. Please call me Midas."

"Thank you for welcoming me into your fine city." Alexander raised an eyebrow at Black Cleitus, surprised at the simplicity of the greeting.

"Indeed," Midas grinned, "Come now, the baths have been drawn and you must be weary from your ride. Dinner will be served in the main hall."

Alexander dismounted. He was followed in suit by the rest of his team. Releasing Buchephalus to the stable hands that appeared, he followed Gordius up the stairs and into the palace. The floors were well worn and smooth. Tall pillars ran along the lengths of the entrance giving an excellent view over the city and mountain ranges. As they walked through the guarded giant entry doors, the scenery changed. Billowing sheers played on the breezes and rich scents filled the air assuaging the senses. Alexander noted that the Midas greeted every servant that passed him with the warm welcome, like a family member.

"I hope you will find these quarters up to your standards," the Midas smiled.

"Your kindness holds no boundaries," Alexander said

entering the room and eyeing the women filling the bath on the platform in the rear of the room. Their bosoms heaved as they laughed. Water kissed their skin as they filled the bath. The wet fabric was scarce, and could not hide the bounty it was designed to restrain. Alexander couldn't help but stare at the plump bottom lip of one, and the long sweeping eyelashes of the other.

Once the entourage was alone, and the gracious smiles of courtesy had fallen, Alexander stood in the middle of the room gazing at the servant women until they giggled and blushed. He was sure they knew of his intent. Cleitus positioned the men to guard around the room. Alexander drew his eyes from the women to his guards, noting that Cleitus stood on the ledge overlooking a sheer drop.

"All is as it should be?" Alexander returned his focus to the bath and waiting women.

"It is, Sire."

"Then I will bathe." He walked over to the waiting women and held his arms outward. As he expected, they rushed forward and began to undo the clasps and gatherings of his armor, peeling it off him layer by layer. "See what you can find out while you are about, Cleitus."

Alexander didn't see Cleitus bow in dismissal, but he vaguely heard the rustle of fabrics signifying his exit. The water was warm and as inviting as the women. He relaxed under their expert hands. The women kneaded every muscle paying special attention to the muscles knotted by battle scars. The water itself was a luxury that he had missed during his travel between conquests. The mere feeling of the warm liquid enveloping his body was exhilarating. The two pliant bodies next to him rubbing him down was more than any man could be thankful for. He could feel desire rising within him, a need to be sated that only a woman could provide. He ran his hands over their young bodies drawing shrieks and giggles from them. They were soft, yielding, and warm. The ride had been long. Alexander smiled; these two would be well worth the chase.

Alexander lay with his head against the stone side of the tub. His eyes still in an unseeing stare.

"Sire?"

Alexander jerked from his thoughts, turning his head at the urgency in Cleitus' voice. "Is all well?"

"From this angle you looked... too still."

"I have been sated." Alexander chuckled. The two women emerged from the depths of the water giggling. "That will be all, thank you ladies." He chuckled again and slapped the women on their rumps sending them shrieking out of the bath.

He rose and stepped out of the bath reaching for his robe, noting that Cleitus had also bathed. He glanced at the guards who had not yet had an opportunity of down time. "Rotate them out and we will talk."

Cleitus motioned to the guards, who filed out of the room; only two remained at the door opening.

Alexander rummaged through the clothes that had been laid out for him. Nothing in the palace spoke of extreme lavishness. Everything was clean and practical. This made his clothing appear outlandish. He opted for a basic tunic inlaid with as minimal gold as he could find from his trunk. "So what news do you bear?" he asked of Cleitus. His voice was hushed, not knowing who may have an interest in his conversation.

"I am told that the old King Gordius, neither inherited nor conquered this land for the throne, rather, he was aided by an Oracle."

"Really? I will be sure to ask the current King about this Oracle this very eve." Alexander mused, "Was any other information shared with you?"

"The cart at the temple doorway is the same cart that King Gordius rode into town with. He offered it to Zeus, and it has sat there for 100 years waiting for someone. "

"A strange offering, no? Who is this someone?"

"Well, the story goes on to say that the same Oracle has foretold the man who loosens the knot holding the staves will rule all of Asia."

"Is that so?" Alexander rubbed his chin thoughtfully with his fingertips, "so the cart has sat in that same position for 100 years?"

"So they say, Sire."

"And naught has sought to loosen the knot?"

"In truth, Sire, many have tried and failed."

"This is a challenge that I must undertake," Alexander whirled about to face Cleitus.

"Sire, if you fail?"

"I cannot fail," Alexander smiled."

"Sire, many have tried. Perhaps there is something about this knot that does not permit it to be loosened."

Alexander glanced at the concern in his friend's eyes, feeling nothing but confidence rise against the doubt. "I will loosen it! They will all see that I will rule the world." He drew up to his full height and raised his fist at the ceiling in assurance as he emphasized his self-proclaimed fate.

"Sire, you are undefeated already."

Alexander looked at the anxious face of his comrade, "Cleitus, worry not. For this will be my destiny, to rule the world. This omen will work in my favor. I must see this Oracle and hear the foretelling of my good fortune."

"Sire have a care—" Black Cleitus started.

Alexander thumped his comrade at arms on the back in reassurance, "No victory that we have claimed to this day has been decisively ours. When I loosen this legendary knot, it will be known that I am the one foretold to rule all, and Asia will just be the beginning. This message will reach all ears of friend and foe alike. They will know that the message was not of my making alone, the Oracle has also foreseen my victory! Mark my words Black Cleitus, this day will be ours."

Alexander watched Black Cleitus purse his lips and nod his head. He patted him on the back once again, this time with vigor, "Come, dear friend, worry not. For now, let us fill our bellies and satisfy all our desires."

With his arm still around Cleitus' shoulder, the two marched forward towards the great hall. Alexander jibed about his earlier conquest with the two supple women who had met his every need, until his olfactory senses were assaulted by rich, savory scents of meats laced with herbs and spices. A cup of sweet wine was pressed into his hand and he was waved into a seat by the King of Phrygia. The dining area looked like the sparring pit now had a dual purpose. The sides were lined with pillows and lavish throws for royalty at one end over the four stairs leading into the pit. The pit floor was covered with sand. Bare feet dancers moved their bodies in fabric that incensed the dullest imagination to the beat of the intoxicating music.

"Come, come friend, sit and eat," the Midas laughed.

Alexander noted the King's voice already betrayed a level of inebriation. He was sure to spill more wine than he drank to press information from him. Alexander laughed and made grand gestures with his hands, spilling his wine and laughing often. Each time he brought the chalice to his lips; he no more than wet them. The heady juice scarcely made it passed his lips. The taut bellies and ample breasts shaken and flaunted in front of him were no cause for distraction; Alexander was after information.

"Your city thrives well," he commented, as a young woman refilled his chalice.

"We are a humble people that have followed the teachings of Gordius and the fates have been kind to us."

"This name Gordius, I am not familiar with his story." Alexander buried his left arm as he leaned into the pillows. His right hand played with his Chalice, as he stared at the dark life impairing liquid.

"Ah, King Gordius was no more than a peasant when he met with the Oracle. One day, an eagle landed on his cart, which he took to be a sign. The eagle did not stray when he began towards the town. The Oracle told the people of Phrygia, who were without a King, that their future King would come to them in a wagon. When Gordius arrived in his oxcart, he was made King. He was a humble man, and so offered his oxcart to Zeus, tying the staves with a decidedly peculiar knot. The Oracle then foretold that whosoever untied the knot would rule all of Asia."

Alexander had stopped twirling his chalice. He watched the Midas staring at him. He held a strange twinkle in his eye and knew that the man before him was no more inebriated than he. They each had played the same façade to measure the other.

He tilted his head back and drank his full of the sweet wine. Looking deep into the eyes of the Midas, he placed the empty chalice on the stone, "I would like to see this Oracle."

Alexander watched the smile deepen across the King of Phrygia's face, "I knew that you would not be able to resist the challenge."

"The fates have already ordained my destiny," Alexander grinned, "This Oracle of yours will only be validating that I am the one."

"We shall see my friend," the Midas jumped to his feet.

Alexander laughed, "The night is mine, my friend. Is it not fitting that as a son of Zeus, that I be the one to become worthy of the claim?"

The music stopped, and Alexander looked at the King. A quick glance around the room told him that all eyes were on the Phrygian King, too. He raised his eyebrows in question, lifting his empty chalice to spur the decision.

"People of Phrygia and visiting Macedonians, we go to the Oracle and then onto the Temple of Zeus. King Alexander will take a turn at untying the knot on the cart of Gordius."

Cheers and gasps echoed around the halls. Alexander matched his stride to the gait of the King of Phrygia. He glanced at Midas, adjusting the length of his stride to stay abreast of the Phrygian King. For a shorter, rotund man, he knew how to manipulate his body to walk at a fast pace.

The entourage started up the stairs towards the Temple of Zeus. The Oracle was located at the midpoint. Alexander drew deep breaths, steadying each one to control the heaving of his chest. He smiled at the rotund King, who was bent over leaning on the brick wall for support. He knew that King Midas felt more than a mere burn searing through his chest.

"Shall we?" Alexander motioned to Midas, who was still gulping volumes of air. He moved forward when the other King nodded, and entered the dark crack in the mountainside. An inky blackness enveloped him, touching his skin with cold, silky fingers. As he felt his way along the rocky cavern, the path became illuminated. His skin prickled, feeling the absence of touch. Alexander checked behind him to ensure Midas was following him. The King waved him onwards. Looking ahead, he could see a circular stone pit. Caution slowed his step as he moved forward.

"I wish I had my sword," he muttered.

"You don't need one, it's only the Oracle here," Midas responded.

"Where Oracles are concerned, nothing is safe." Alexander answered.

"Alexander, Alexander, Alexander," voices echoed around the cavern.

He spun around in the direction of the echoing voices before returning his attention to the center of the stone pit, where he could now see a young, naked woman lying. Trails of smoke wreathed its way around her body like a serpent. Her eyes were a piercing violet. Her skin was translucent, appearing as if it had never been kissed by the sun, and her dark auburn hair moved in its own tempest. Every facet of the Oracle's body was perfect. Her small breasts had never suckled or felt the weight of life giving sustenance. They sat like little orbs high on her chest, the aureole like unblinking eyes. Her doe-like violet eyes held allure; Alexander felt his eyes locked in with hers. His body responded with a primal want and need. He fought against her pull. Her body rose and she writhed to an unknown rhythm.

"Alexander?"

He turned his head to find Black Cleitus shaking him. Looking down, his foot was braced against the rim of the stone pit and his muscles were clenched. Relaxing, he nodded to Black Cleitus and returned his gaze to the Oracle, who stared down at him from her suspended position.

"You have questions, Alexander?" The question came from the Oracle though her lips never moved.

He pondered upon the curvature of her voluptuous lips, "Indeed. I have many."

"Only the answer to one may be yours."

"My mission is to conquer the known world. I would have you proclaim it mine." Alexander grinned.

"At the temple of Zeus lies an oxcart with staves bound by a knot. The man to loosen the knot will rule all of Asia. Fulfill the prophecy and the proclamation is yours."

"What did I tell you?" Midas thumped Alexander on his back.

As he turned away from the Oracle, Alexander noticed the flames extinguishing as she slipped back into her slumber. He felt a sense of peace wash over him.

"What happened to you back there?" Black Cleitus asked.

"Your timing was good, brother," Alexander gripped Cleitus' arm.

"The Oracle is a lonely woman and her grip is strong. I was surprised that you made it so long. Most young men like you don't last," the Midas grinned.

Black Cleitus reached for his sword.

"Stay your weapon Black Cleitus; I knew the risk of seeing the Oracle. The King is right, most young men don't last, but I'm not like others; I am a son of Zeus." Alexander thumped Midas and Black Cleitus on their backs.

At the top of the hill Alexander walked to the oxcart, curiosity spurring him onward. He had never encountered a challenge he couldn't face. "This cart is ancient." Alexander laughed, as he examined it. "It looks as if it is standing by the sheer grace of Zeus alone." He drew laughter from the growing crowd.

Bending down, he examined the weathered rope. From years of exposure to weather, the fibers had become one solid mass, swelling into their current position. The knot itself was well fashioned with the ends of the knot hidden deep within the knot's own folds; hiding the nature of the knot's beginning or end. Alexander spent a little time tugging on various parts of it. Brittle top fibers broke off in his hands. He rubbed them between his thumb and forefinger. A moss like growth covered the aged rope like a coating of sealant. He could hear the whispers in the crowd amassing. After some time and mild frustration, Alexander stepped back and placed his arm across his body like a shelf. He rested his elbow on his arm to rub his chin with his fingertips. A quick smile flashed across his face before he yelled, "What does it matter how I loose it?" In a flash, he pulled Black Cleitus' sword from its sheath and in a single swift motion slashed the knot separating the staves. The wheels collapsed inward and the cart's end sat on the ground with a thud. A plume of dust signaled the demise of the cart's long standing position.

The crowd gasped as Alexander held Black Cleitus' sword high into the air proclaiming, "Hear me now, I note this day that I, Alexander, a son of Zeus, have fulfilled the Oracle's prophecy." Lightning crackled from the sky and within the temple.

Alexander turned and saluted Zeus in the skies, closing his eyes as the winds blew, carrying the cheers of his victory to his ears.

CHAPTER ONE

Alex walked out of the rift that he tapped into, to transport him from the Macedo Ink tower in New York City to the beach front home in sunny South Florida.

"I don't know how you can stand living here. The sun roasts all that dare to walk in its rays even while it is setting." Alex laughed, as he walked down the open staircase spying his age old friend Leonidas at the wet bar pouring a drink. "That is one angry ball of fire in the sky."

"Ah, Lex, what a surprise…"

Alex froze on the bottom step of the staircase at the use of his public name and stared at Leonidas who turned slowly. "Why is that old friend?" Alex used all his preternatural senses to feel for any danger that could cause his friend to response with such a human greeting.

"I didn't expect you up so early," Leonidas tilted his head and flicked open his index finger, middle finger and ring finger.

"Ah." Alex nodded, understanding that at least three people were listening in. He moved with a casual air that belied any predatory reflexes. "You know I like to watch a good sun set. Florida has some picturesque evenings." Alex dropped his voice, and in vampiric tongue beyond the realm of human hearing and discovery, he asked, "What the fuck is going on, Leo?"

"I've had humans staking out my house all day long."

"What do they want?"

"I'm guessing that they are following up on the file that was leaked."

"Do we have any idea of what's at stake and the ramifications of our exposure?"

"They've been discussing the details all day. They have no idea who gave them the file, but they have my name and tracers for some of the shell companies that I used to move your money around, as well as a few others."

"But it's real money, not illegal funds." Alex eased into the contemporary sofa thinking it was a tad hard for his liking. He accepted the drink offered by Leonidas.

"To them, it will be all and the same. This money has been around for thousands of years as you know Alexander, but to these humans, whose minds cannot fathom such depths, these shell companies are a trigger for illegal money laundering. In fact, some of the same schemes may indeed be used to keep the money current. If I didn't, you would be running around trying to trade Spanish bullion."

"I hear gold is still trading well." Alex laughed taking a pull from his glass.

"Seriously?"

Alex checked his mirth against Leonidas' scorn," Okay, so I'm not being serious and I understand the situation."

"So how do you want to handle it?"

"I'm thinking up a strategy right now."

"We can always call them in and eat them." Leonidas laughed.

"Right," Alex grinned.

"Ah, I long for the old days."

"Which old days are those? The ones where we sat as Kings in simpler times, or when we hunted humans as prey before growing a conscience?"

Alex watched Leonidas' impassive face break into a smile.

"The ones where, as a vampire, I could do whatever the fuck I wanted without question."

"You've spent the better part of this millennium in solitude. Aren't you up for a change of scenery?" Alex asked, taking another sip of blood.

"I am indeed." Leonidas responded. "Before all of this

happened I had asked the council to consider decentralizing the system; they resisted. A millennium of solitude is enough of a personal contribution."

"So why don't you take a bullet." Alexander laughed, "I'm going to allow them to take me. We have to draw out the leak. This is getting way out of hand."

"Are you sure you'll be able to handle a human jail, Alexander? There must be another way?"

"I've never turned down a challenge, Leo, you should know that. Besides, better a human jail than a vampiric one. And it's not just me that's at risk. While I would like to preserve everything that I've built, the entire lifestyle of all vampires is at stake should the humans decide to launch an investigation."

"You are older and wiser now. There's no need to run off half-cocked."

Alexander laughed, "You leave my cock out of this. Besides, I had Asia in my palm back then. Now that I'm older and wiser, as you say, drawing out the thorn in my side should be a ride in the park. What's more, look who's talking—who was it that took three-hundred some odd men and made a stand against Xerxes?"

Leonidas rubbed his eyebrow, "Okay, I guess you weren't the only one running around half-cocked, but like I said, we're older and wiser."

"Definitely older," Alex sank into the chair, "I want you in

New York. Figure out how to save my money. Talk to Max, my son, and help him find that damned hole. I want it plugged. See my wife, Lina, and kiss the baby for me. Tell her I need to finish this and then I'll be home and to please hold the fort."

"A wife and children, huh," Leonidas scratched his eyebrow deep in contemplation, "I have watched your birth, death, and second birth. Never have I seen you like this. The Great Alexander has been domesticated, I am quite intrigued."

"The path I'm about to walk is a dangerous one, as it will leave me vulnerable and exposed. I worry for my family as well."

"I will watch over them."

"They will make your task difficult, Leo," Alex scratched his head, "Jack, aka Jacqui Brunson. She is very human, and more so she is the Peace Keeper between up, down, and terra."

"Really?" Leonidas sat forward, "I've always wanted to see one up close."

"Yeah, well, her boyfriend and Light's Warrior is none other than Miguel."

"Miguel?"

"Michael, the Archangel."

"You've got to be kidding me," Leonidas took a large gulp of his blood drink, swirling the contents at the bottom of his glass to stop the coagulation of the liquid. "You've been living quite the life."

"I suppose I should mention that Lina is Catalina De Diablo."

Leonidas put his glass down on the table, "The crowned Prince of Darkness herself, and together you have managed offspring."

"Max was my human adoptive son, but an incident occurred at the tower forcing me to turn him; Archimedes, he is ours yes, and quite a handful."

"Alexander, I had no idea that your life was so full."

"The source of this leak has me quite curious, Leo"

"Why is that?"

"The source claims to know of you, but they can't be all that knowledgeable as they spelled your name wrong. Well, they used your current human profile. Why do that if you are exposing the vampiric lifestyle?"

"So, not an ancient?"

"Agreed; maybe affiliated with one, but not an ancient."

Alex watched Leonidas put up his hand. This was one vampire that he trusted with all his being. Leonidas transformed into the old man people knew as Leonides Brown; Alex trained his ears. The squelch of the radio always irritated his ears; after listening, he was quite sure that humans were going for an attempt at entry. He bulked up to become Lex Macedo, his public alias. Leaning back into the sofa he waited; only this time, not as the hunter, but as the hunted.

The sun had fully dipped behind the horizon allowing darkness to dominate. Alex flexed his muscles sinking into the seat, feeling the supremacy of the night wash over him like a wave of power. He disliked the pending lack of control that he would have over the situation. He reached out, forming a telepathic link with Max while staring at Leonidas.

Max?

Dad?

Some shit is about to go down. I'm in Florida and don't have much time to explain. I want you to figure out how to create a paper trail proving that I flew down to Florida no more than twenty-four hours ago.

What's going on?

No time to explain right now, I have to focus on keeping Lex's image intact. I'll reach out to you and Lina later. I'm going to be arrested for money laundering.

Holy shit, Dad! That's not good.

I know—and Max?

Yeah?

One more thing, fucking plug that hole so nothing like this happens again.

Already done. I'll be waiting for your contact.

Alex felt the link close, although his oldest friend sat across from him, a feeling of emptiness crept into the pit of his belly. He wondered if his enemies had felt like this during the onset of battle. He could hear the intense whispers of the task force increasing. The rustle of fabrics, the click of heavy artillery, and the hushed footfalls as they attempted stealth against two of the most lethal vampires and military strategists the world had ever known.

A smile crept across his face knowing that if either he or Leonidas wanted to, they could crush this small task force in a single heartbeat. His smile faded. He wondered exactly what they had become. Leonidas was about to take a bullet, as well as change identities and he, well, he was about to allow himself to become the most vulnerable and exposed vampire in all of history.

"Ready?" Leonidas asked in vampiric tongue.

Alex nodded. A canister of gas bounced into the room making a clinking noise against the tile every time the edge made contact with the tile. Until it lost momentum and rolled, hissing its obnoxious contents into the air in a spiraling, smoky plume. He chugged the rest of the blood pooling at the bottom of his glass. As if on command, Leonidas reached forward and picked up the large remote from the glass table positioned between the two couches that flanked the walls. Alex nodded, encouraging Leonidas to proceed.

He grimaced as the sparks flared. Explosions could be heard in the extremities of the house. Shots were fired. Alex shook his head. Preparing for the worst, he looked over at Leonidas and guessed that his sentiments were about the same. This exercise was going to be a true test of his control and resolve.

Leonidas stood up in his form of an elderly man and began

yelling. Smoke swirled around his form moving like an eerie unnatural fog, as he moved towards the stairway. The members of the task force came burgeoning down the stairway yelling and screaming for everyone to freeze; but Leonidas kept moving towards them. The wet bar exploded, and one anxious task force member pulled on the trigger. Alex curled his lip and closed his eyes. Vampire or not, bullets hurt, and were a royal pain to have removed. He saw Leonidas' body crumple to the floor. His head lolled on the tumbled marble in a pool of welling blood.

"Don't shoot," Alex yelled in his best Lex Macedo voice. "What on earth are you doing in here? Who are you? Why are you shooting?"

The task force collected around him. Men barked orders from within their masks. Alex stared down the barrels of several SAR21s some equipped with Round Corner Firing modules. He focused on a bead of sweat trickling down the forehead under the mask of the task force leader. Without warning, the wet bar exploded again. Slivers of glass flew like shrapnel. Alex shielded his face. One of the task force members fell to the ground yelling. The metallic scent of blood overpowered the scent of gas. Alex controlled the primal urge to consider the man prey and suck him dry.

Hands tugged him out of his seat. A low growl escaped his lips. Trained guns were moments away from his forehead. Yet, none of that mattered. He knew he could kill them all without taxing his brain, or lifting a talon. Still, he allowed himself to be dragged out of the mansion. His knee grazed on the rough concrete. Once outside, he was thrown to the ground, his hands tied crudely with zip straps behind his back. He felt grains of dirt pressing into his face. Desperation provoked his ire. He stared at the soles of the boots at his eye level to maintain his waning resolve. He could feel the onset of the change and struggled to quiet his inner beast, reminding himself of the choices he made. Hands tugged at him again, picking him up off the ground. As a human, the gas was supposed to irritate his eyes and lungs. Alex coughed.

He closed his eyes hearing the explosions echo around the house. Without looking, he knew that the entire house was on fire. *Leonidas?* Alex searched mentally for his old friend. He pursed his lips hoping he'd gotten out. While a bullet wouldn't kill Leo, fire could. Alex stared at the house from the tinted windows of the unmarked police car he had been placed in. By focusing on the two men, he could hear the heated argument between the task force leader and the rear of a very familiar shape. He narrowed his eyes, allowing his brain to absorb the cadence of the voice, the style of dress, and the greasy, slicked back hair.

"What is Ed Trattoria doing here?" Alex mused. "He doesn't look as if he is working on my behalf."

Reaching out to Max, he connected telepathically. *Max?*

Yeah, Dad?

Are you by Jack?

Yeah, she's right here. Are you okay?

Not really, I've been detained. I'm sitting in the back of an unmarked police vehicle with zip straps restraining my hands. I would love nothing more than to crush all of them, but we need to figure out the source of this attack. I want the source eliminated.

Where do we start?

Ed Trattoria is here, curious enough.

Trattoria? Isn't that Jack's old boyfriend?

Yes.

What's he doing there?

I don't know. He hasn't come to talk to me yet. I'm just watching him have it out with the task force leader. I think these are folks from FATF. At least that's what I think I can make out on their backs without going into their minds.

Then they are going to question you on financial fraud or money laundering for sure.

I'm guessing that to be the case, as Leonidas is involved and all he does is guard our money. Listen, have Jack call the greasy Detective right now.

And say what?

Invite him over for dinner or something.

The objective?

I want to know what he's doing here.

Alex watched Trattoria reach into his right blazer pocket and extract his cell phone. He stared through the tinted glass as the detective turned to look towards him. The level of tint in the glass was beyond regulation; Ed Trattoria couldn't see him. His voice became clear as Alex blocked out all other sounds. His followed him as he moved away from the task force leader.

"Jack, what a surprise—no, no it's good to hear from you. I thought you were still mad at me over the lockup and parking ticket thing. Oh I would love to have dinner, but can I have a rain check? I'm out of town right now… you know I can't discuss police business with you. No, I don't know how long I'll be here. What's keeping me? I won't go into details, but let's just say I warned you about the friends you keep… no not Alex. I haven't found anything on him yet. Strange enough it's his brother. Jack, I've told you way too much. I gotta go, sweetness… yeah me too. I'll call you when I get back in town.

Max

Yeah, Dad

Someone has to be feeding that man information. He doesn't have the tools to find anything on us. Yet he's discovered something on Lex? I think that's strange. Lex has the cleanest profile.

I'll look into it.

Gotta go, he's coming.

Alex settled back into the luxury leather seat of the Yukon and focused on maintaining his Lex Macedo profile.

The door opened.

"Mr. Macedo?"

"You sound unsure?" Alex turned to face Trattoria, as much as the restraints would allow.

"Mr. Lex Macedo."

"Hmmm, I would shake your hand, but I've been restrained for some reason unbeknownst to me. Aren't you the detective that assisted me when my building was experiencing difficulty with the fire alarm? What are you doing in Florida?"

"Yes, Ed Trattoria, sir, and you weren't read your rights?"

"No. One moment I was drinking bourbon with an old friend, and the next I'm finding that your friends have shot up the building, killed my friend, and his house is now on fire. I've been thrown on the floor, restrained, and forgotten about in this vehicle."

Alex furrowed his brows as Trattoria slammed the door close. He heard him yell to the task force leader. "No one read this guy his fucking rights?"

Moments later, the door opened again. Alex raised his eyebrows as Ed Trattoria proceeded to Mirandize him and then shut the door again.

CHAPTER TWO

"What did he say?" Max asked, casting his eyes upward as the elevator sounded its arrival.

"He kinda danced around not wanting to tell me anything. He reminded me that he warned me about the friends I keep. You heard me ask why he has it in for Alex. He told me that they're after Alex's brother," Jack answered.

"That would be Lex." Max swirled his tongue over the smooth surface of the plastic retainer covering his canines. A smile crept over his face. He remembered when his girlfriend, Sam, a TruBlood witch and owner of La Sangre de Vida— a flourishing blood bank servicing the upper echelon of the vampiric realm—put them on when he became a newly turned vampire. Though almost a year had passed, control was still an issue he had to work on and he was still considered a fledgling. Most of the people that he loved dearly were human; he wasn't willing to give up the lifestyle he was accustomed to, so wearing a retainer was a small compromise.

"Hmmm," Jack raised a thoughtful finger to rest on her lower lip, "When did Alex go down to Florida?"

"Today." The voice filtered down from above.

Max glanced at Jack whose eyes were following Lina down the stair case. He had been so deep in thought, it hadn't dawned on him that the bell indicating the arrival of the elevator would mean that someone else would be joining them. "Hi, Lina," he sank deeper into the leather couch, thankful to see it was just his step-mother.

"What's going on Max?"

He looked at Lina who sat across from both Jack and himself forming a triangle.

"Have you spoken to Dad?"

"I just did, he suggested that I get with the two of you and figure out what's going on."

Max watched Lina hang her head in her hands. "Where is Archi?"

"He's with the sitter." Lina smiled.

"Wow that sounds so normal. Like no one would know that the sitter was a killer wood nymph. Or better yet, that folks would misconstrue a nymph meaning a sex freak." Jack shook her head. "Okay. So what do we know?" Jack jumped off the couch and began pacing. "We know that Ed has some information."

"Yeah, but he didn't uncover it himself." Max interjected.

"So we believe. He also has to be working with a task force of some sort," Jack mused.

"Why is that?" Lina queried.

"Because he wouldn't have the jurisdiction to make an arrest in Florida; he only has limited jurisdiction here in New York City." Jack whirled around and continued pacing.

"What agencies could be researching Lex?" Max pondered.

"The Federal Bureau of Investigations might have cause, or the Financial Action Task Force could be if it's an international thing," Jack turned to pace in the opposite direction, "I mean there are just so many avenues."

"Dad did mention the FATF. Said he saw those letters on the backs of some of the action force that swarmed the house. There has to be a trail. I don't understand how Dad, Lex rather, makes it down to Florida for less than how long Lina, before he is swept up in this nonsense? It's not like he took public transportation which set off the bells and whistles. His form of transportation has no electronic signature anyone human could trace." Frustration was evident in Max's expression.

"Not even an hour." Lina looked at her cell phone to check

the time.

"Then it's all circumstantial," Jack sat on the couch, "there's no way they were anticipating that Lex was a part of their investigation at this point. They must have been investigating whomever he went to visit. Who did he go to visit anyway?"

"Leonidas." Lina shook her head. Her tresses tumbled about her shoulders.

"That doesn't mean anything to me," Jack laughed, "I'm not well versed in the paranormal super-pages."

"Uh, Leonidas was King of the Spartans, most people know of him because of the movie that just came out: The 300?"

Lina raised her eyebrows at Jack looking for some recognition of understanding. Max wondered if she were going to spell it out any further. Jack seemed quite ignorant on history.

"Yikes, how was I to know that this Leonidas was the same one. Give me a break. I mean your son is called Archimedes. You wouldn't expect anyone to think that he was the original Archimedes from like 200BC or something." Jack got up to pace again and stuck her hands in her back pockets.

"She has a point," Max turned to Lina. "Well this Leonidas is the one that people know of. He is our money mover."

"What does that mean?" Jack asked.

"When you are immortal you can't live in the same location the whole time. People start to get suspicious because we never age," Lina started, "so we have an organized fashion for moving about."

"What's that?" Jack paused.

"We are all assigned territories which change periodically within a given region."

"So during those changes there's always someone like Leonidas that tracks and moves the money for us. We don't have to be poverty stricken after each move." Max interjected.

"Why would you lose money?" Jack stopped in front of Max.

"Don't forget that we often have to change identities when we move." Max's voice faded as thoughts of the future permeated his focus. He wondered how his life with Sam would take shape. Lina's voice snapped him back into the conversation.

"…We need to get him out of there. I'm ready to go there and just blow the whole place up," Lina pointed at Jack, "I'll have no pity for your little friend either. He is fucking with the wrong family."

Max focused on Lina. She had become quite still, like the calm before the storm. When she looked up, her eyes held contempt for all who would dare to cross her. She looked beyond cold and calculating.

"You can't just blow the place up," Jack furrowed her brows.

"I can too." Lina stood up.

Max jumped off the couch and placed a soothing hand on Lina's forearm. "I don't think she means that you can't, like not within your powers can't; but maybe that you shouldn't." He tried to pass along a feeling of calm. "I also don't think that's what Dad would want." He added once he felt Lina de-escalate.

"I do think that you should go down there, though," Jack mused.

"You do?" Lina turned.

"I do. I think we need to engage lawyers and I also think that you need to go down there to see Alex like a normal wife would."

"Hold on, you're forgetting that it's not Alexander Macedo that has been arrested," Max held up his handshaking his head; "we have to respond as if he is Lex Macedo the head of the Macedo Ink."

"No problem, Mijo," Lina crossed her legs and rested her head in the palm of her created elbow nest, "I'll go down there as Alexander Macedo."

"You can do that?" Max asked in unison with Jack. A quick glance in Jack's direction made him wonder if he were wearing the same incredulous look as she was.

"Well, I might need some assistance to sustain the image. If Alejandro can image Lex, I should be able to image him. I hope I know his mannerisms well enough to portray him to others."

"Holy shit Lina," Max laughed.

"When I go down there what are you two going to do?" Lina asked.

"I think we should figure out who the players are and who

dropped this in Ed's lap." Max knit his brows. It'll be good that you'll be down there. We may need some answers."

"Good, I'll be there tomorrow then." Lina folded her arms.

"You can't just appear there. You will have to travel by conventional means and in synch with a scheduled event, court date or something. We need to be able to show a trail. Let's not forget that part of what we are hiding is our human factor, or lack of." Max wondered how long Alex could maintain his façade in a prison setting.

"That's an excellent point Max; we need to know what's going on. We have to find a way of getting into their heads," Jack slumped into the armchair matching the leather couch, "I feel like so much is out of our control right now."

Max watched Jack's leg dangle over the side of the armchair. His eyes followed the panther tattoo that was prowling its way down her leg. He couldn't help but crack a smile as he watched it hiss at Lina as she paced by Jack. "We'll get our hands around it all. Don't worry Jack," Max gave his best attempt at reassurance, though he wondered how deep his belief ran. Would they all come out on top? Alex could get out if he wanted to, and yet he was choosing to expose himself. For what? Was this the best way to go about figuring out who was trying to annihilate the Macedo Empire?

A loud noise broke Max's thoughts. He jumped up ripping his retainer out of his mouth baring his fangs.

"Easy," Lina appeared by his side and placed a restraining hand on him. "It's just Miguel."

Max nodded, replacing the retainer. He ran his tongue over his canines and willed them back until they were normal by human standards and the retainer resumed its snug fit. His fingers found his hair.

"Your skin feels a little damp," Lina smiled, "Would you mind getting me a glass of something refreshing, maybe A or B+?"

"Sure," Max found himself mumbling and thought he should have some himself. The signs of hunger were not always as clear, and by the time the thirst reared its ugly head it was usually too late.

He heard Jack run towards Miguel. A glance over his shoulder told him they were immersed in an embrace. He wondered what Sam was doing. A whole day had passed since he'd last seen her. They had been missing each other due to her new schedule of commitments at Las Sangre de Vida and his new lifestyle requirements. He loved his penthouse suite and his ability to retain his near human lifestyle. Becoming a vampire meant a bunch of sacrifices, most of which meant not seeing Sam much. But, the fact his suite was already setup for a vampire meant he could keep most of his routine status quo.

The staircase from the elevator wound its way down next to the kitchen, turning at the last moment to exit the entrance towards the open seating area. The kitchen, with its smooth, contemporary feel, was setup to be a central point, and from there, his view extended as far as the eye could see through his ceiling-to-floor digital windows. The windows held a special skin within the double pane that responded to tiny cameras placed in each corner. Each window was networked to the next so that all of them in the penthouse condo were linked to the computer infrastructure. This meant that Max automatically had a UV filter on all windows, as well as the capability to ratchet back the intensity of the sun when it was too bright. It allowed him to experience the sun in some form and fashion.

Max kept a watchful eye on Miguel and Jack as he reached beneath the counter for a fresh bottle of A+ and popped the cork. The metallic aroma wafted to his nostrils. As if on automatic pilot, he inhaled another draft of the freshly released scents. He could smell the heparin infused in the blood as an anticoagulant to allow the bottle to remain shelf stable. Pouring the viscous substance into two waiting crystal glasses, he listened to the exchange between Jack and Miguel, otherwise known as Michael the Archangel and Warrior of Light.

"Where were you?" he heard Jack asked.

"I went to Florida on a suspicion," Miguel answered.

"A suspicion?"

"Yes. I've been watching Ed Trattoria for a while now."

"Why?"

Miguel shifted on his feet, "Let's just say I was checking out the competition."

"Competition? Oh my goodness," Jack covered her mouth, "you were jealous?"

"Perhaps, but then I started noticing things."

"What kind of things?"

"A soucouyant paid a visit to the precinct and dropped off a packet of information with the word Leonides on it."

"Leonides? Jack turned to Max, "isn't that the name of Alex's friend?"

"Almost, his name is Leonidas." Max mumbled, allowing the blood to run over his taste buds to savor it. "But that doesn't mean much because they all change their public aliases so often that a minor name change may not be of significant consequence. We still may be talking about the same Leonidas if that's where Alex got arrested." He re-corked the bottle returning it to the chiller which maintained a consistent temperature.

"I wonder if that means anything." Jack pulled on her bottom lip. "Go on Mig, perhaps something will give us a clue as to who is behind all this. Then we'll be able to get Alex home quicker."

"The documentation that was given to Ed held traces of the shell companies that have been used by the Macedo family to protect their wealth over the years. I'm not sure how far back it goes. I do know that Ed Trattoria suspects money laundering. He was poking around making some inquiries and then was contacted by the Financial Action Task Force. From what I could make out, the FATF has a bigger file with more than just Macedo money under investigation."

"Hmmm, so this has gone global." Jack pulled on her lip making a popping sound.

Max gave her a disapproving look.

She apologized.

A wave of power crashed over him like an ocean wave that any surfer would be honored to try and ride. Turning, he found the source to be Lina. She appeared to be stewing.

"What's wrong?" Max asked offering her the requested glass of blood.

"That little man gives me the creeps." Lina spat. "I want to possess him. Make all of this work in our favor somehow and then kill him." She sipped at the glass.

"Who? Ed Trattoria?" Max glanced at Jack wondering what she ever saw in the greasy New York detective.

"I definitely think that we need to find a way to help him, so he's working in our favor."

Max shook his head. "I'm not thinking Dad wants us to do anything rash. He could have killed the entire task force if he wanted to, I'm sure of it. He could tip the balance in his favor at any time, but he's gotta be riding it out until we figure out the source of the attacks. This has been going on way too long and if we retaliate now then he loses everything, has to start again, and it'll be more difficult to figure out who did this when we are at the bottom of the deck of cards."

Max watched Lina fold her arms and pout, though she seemed to simmer down. Satisfied that he had won the battle for the day, he turned back to Miguel, "Anything else?"

"You are right; Alex did go and see Leonidas. The task force entered his home just as he got there. I could hear them talking in the vampiric tongue of the ancients. I saw Leonidas get shot."

"So you haven't cracked that yet?" Max laughed, watching a scowl take residence on Miguel's tan face. The angel's platinum, spiky hair made his face seem tanner than it usually was. Max now wondered what Jack saw in Miguel. Neither the archangel nor the greasy detective seemed to be Jack's type. If one of them were, Max decided he wouldn't be able to calculate a trend, as the two were so different. The archangel looked like a muscled-bound, inked, gym-head with a less than desirable personality. He appeared angry more often than not, while Trattoria seemed to be his polar opposite. Jack's personality seemed to fit in somewhere between them, although even she had her don't-touch-me and don't-come-near-me moments.

"I have never found a need to learn the tongue of vampires. I am a Warrior of Light and no conversation needs to be had once a vampire has crossed the line."

"So what about Alex?" Jack mused," what happens when he crosses this line of yours?"

"Alex is different. He is my counterpart. A covenant has been exacted and as such, we should be working to a common goal."

"Which is?" Jack flopped on the couch.

"To protect you, of course." Miguel smiled.

Max rolled his eyes, "Great! Now that we have figured out that everyone loves Jack, I think we should divvy up roles so that we can eliminate our threat.

"Wait a minute Max. Miguel, you said you saw Leonidas get shot?" Lina held out her palm.

"I did."

"Shot, not killed?" Lina pursued.

"I'm not certain of his whereabouts. The building burst into flames."

Max and Lina gasped in unison, "Dad?"

"The task force had him detained within the back of a Yukon by the time the building went up in flames."

Max relaxed. Miguel appeared to be quite calm. Then again, he could never tell what was going on in the archangel's head.

"So there was a lapse between the time that Leonidas got shot and the time that the building went up in flames?"

"What are you getting at, Lina?" Max interjected, frustrated that everyone seemed to be dwelling on the fact that the building had burst into flames.

"Leonidas is a very old vampire; he has survived worse than this. If we can find him and talk to him, we will have a clear idea about what we are up against."

Max scanned Lina's face. Her reasoning was sound. "Do you think he knew what was going on?"

Lina laughed. "Of course he did." Max heard sarcasm ran rampant throughout her laugh.

"How can you be sure?" Jack asked.

"It's his job to know everything about the money. Including who is watching it. How do you think the money made it this far? This is not the first time it has been under scrutiny, I'm sure."

"Nor will it be the last time!"

Max turned around to face the source of the strange voice. He found a well-muscled vampire facing him. Brown wavy hair framed his dirt-stained grimy face and a dirty-brown, but otherwise well-maintained beard lined his jaw. He wore a black silk t-shirt that clung to his skin, black pants that spoke of the deft needle of a tailor and black leather Italian shoes.

"You must be Leonidas?"

Max watched as Lina walked forward to greet the newcomer, wishing he had been able to switch gears as fast as she had.

"Indeed I am. You must be Catalina De Diablo?"

"So I am. Please come in and talk with us."

CHAPTER THREE

Alexander sank into the leather seat in rear of the Yukon. Faint scents of chemicals wafted from the seat with each movement. Traces of blood permeated the leather. Faded stains were tell-tale signs of injury or death that had taken place in the very seat in which he sat. The scent of blood, even as old and stale as they were, woke the thirst within him.

The zip straps bit into his wrists. He could smell his own blood now adding to the stale chemical-leached blood in the seats. Pulling his wrists apart with slow measureable strength, he stretched the zip straps until he built some slack. Breathing a sigh of relief, he felt his regenerative properties heal his wounds.

He stared at the sky; the moon was at the crest of her

journey across the midnight blue sea. He had been sitting in the back of the vehicle for hours. Every evening when the sun fell, he reveled in the wash of power that the moon brought. Humans often complained of sun deprivation, could vampires ever be depraved of the silver rays that the moon bequeathed? Not bound like a werewolf, yet still called to revere both in the beauty and power.

Alex sighed. *What the fuck am I doing allowing myself to be taken? I am vulnerable, my family is vulnerable, and yet here I am. This is either the most fucked up decision I have ever made in two thousand plus years, or the most calculating one yet.*

A thump on the roof of the Yukon brought him back from his thoughts. The task leader got into the driver's seat. Alex knitted his brows when Ed Trattoria got into the passenger seat, how had the greasy New York detective become united with this task force leader.

"Ah, a familiar face at least," Alex smiled as Lex would.

"Take the gun."

Alex watched the task leader shove the M16 into Ed Trattoria's hands.

"I don't think I need this."

"You never know when they get violent. Just keep it aimed at him, and we'll be alright."

"You are not a violent man, are you Mr. Macedo?"

Alex raised his eyebrow, "Well, Mr. Trattoria, I have

maintained composure to date. I will say that I have never been provoked to a level of irrationality; but the day is not over."

Alex found himself staring down the barrel of the gun that Trattoria pointed at him.

He could see that his response did not sit well with either of the officers. "Where are we going?" He asked.

"You will be detained at the nearest facility that will take you. Which right now is Dade County?"

"Why?"

"Mr. Macedo, you are wanted on counts of money laundering."

"Is that so?

Trattoria did not respond

"There is a warrant in Florida for this?" Alex pushed.

"You will be extradited back to New York."

"So there is a warrant in New York for this charge?"

"No more questions." The task leader interjected.

Alex stared at the task leader through the rearview mirror, watching with pleasure as he squirmed in his seat under the scrutiny.

He sat back wondering how long each of these processes was going to take. While his absence would force his enemy's hand, there was the slight obstacle about his eating and quarter requirements. He focused on Trattoria, his eyes feeling heavy, as if he were in a lustful trance. He could sense the sweat secreting from Trattoria's glands. Each droplet of perspiration lifted into the air like a bubble filled with hydrogen. Beneath his skin, the pull of blood called. Alex smiled; he had called blood from vampires before, but never humans.

He could feel the blood rising to the surface of the skin. Molecule by molecule Alex called them pulling the blood into the air, forming a faint mist. A smile played at the corner of his lips as the refreshing burst of cloud hit him. *This is how I will survive.* Relieved that his strategy could play through, he stared at Trattoria. He looked like shit. Blue veins were visible under the thin surface of his skin. His normal olive skinned complexion looked gray and ashen. A significant change from when he first stepped into the vehicle. Alex wondered if the task force leader would notice the change in Ed.

The vehicle lurched from a hard right turn. Alex ducked his head to stare between the seats and out the front windshield. A white building illuminated by floodlights loomed out of the night. "Where are we?"

Alex looked at Ed who turned in his seat.

"Why are you even talking to the prisoner?" The task force leader asked, shrugging his shoulders as he turned the wheel to park.

Alex sighed as Ed turned back around.

Using mental persuasion, he sent a message to the task force leader. *Tell Ed where we are!*

"Why would you even feel the need to tell the prisoner that we are at the Justice Center—Dade County lockup?" The task leader went on, throwing the column shifter into park.

"You just told him." Ed twisted in his seat.

Alex settled back, satisfied with the information.

"No," the task force leader looked at Ed from under his eyebrows, "I just told you."

"It's not like he doesn't have ears, you know." Ed mumbled before unclicking his seatbelt.

Alex smiled, watching Ed dismiss the task force leader with a wave of his hand. *What's the matter Ed, no energy to fight? Normally you are a tenacious bull dog.* Alex mused.

A firm grip on his arm and the back of his head rotated him out of the car.

"Out!"

Alex fought the rumble that wanted to explode inside him. No one man had ever been allowed to treat him with such disregard; not in life or his second life. Still, he was here for a purpose. Gritting his teeth and willing back the incisors that had dropped, he bolstered his Lex Macedo facade and straightened up as soon as the task force leader would allow him.

The walk from the vehicle was short. A quick glance told Alex that the task force leader's unit had disbanded. A police officer stood at the ready outside the entry door. Alex watched as the men flashed their badges allowing them entry. The overhead lighting hummed. Some of the bulbs were out, while others flickered in a constant state of neglect.

The march stopped in front of a long desk with a burly sour-faced red-cheek officer. "Warrant number?" The officer didn't look up.

The task force leader cleared his throat, "I am Agent—

"I don't care who you are. I need a warrant number so I know what I'm working with. I don't have all night. No warrant, no arrest, no reason to be here. Let's keep it moving."

Alex tried not to grin. The task force leader reached into his pocket and withdrew folded paperwork and handed it to the burly officer. The paperwork was not received with a smile. Alex understood what was going through the officer's mind without even tapping into it. He had asked for a number and got a piece of paper.

"Prisoner, state your name."

Alex looked into the burly officer's eyes, "Lex Macedo, sir."

"Hmmm," the burly officer squinted into the computer screen and referenced the paper. "Nope, there's no Lex Macedo listed on this warrant, only a Leonides Brown."

Alex watched the burly officer pass the paper back over the counter.

"Process him anyway, I'll get his name added," the task force leader reached into his pocket for his phone.

"Get his name added and then I'll process him. Technically

there's no warrant for him, so there's no reason for him to be here," the burly officer looked into Alex's eyes, "guess it's your lucky day, pal."

Process me. Alex sent the mental suggestion to the burly officer except, he knew that with the force that he applied sending the suggestion it would come across more like a demand. A confused look rest on the burly officer's face. The night was waning; the drain of the sun seemed eminent. Alex wanted to be well within the confines of the facility by the time the Florida sun rose.

The burly officer scratched his head. "What's he in for?"

"Money laundering."

"Felony, huh? Neither of you local?"

"We just need you to hold him pending extradition."

"We're full, but I suppose one more doesn't hurt," the burly officer's fingers flew over the keyboard as if they were in a digital marathon, "Prisoner, place your fingers on the glass."

Alex looked at the glass plate in front of him. He shrugged his shoulders at the questioning eyes of the task force leader. *Hmmm new fingerprinting technology.* After two thousand years, the skin on his fingertips had worn smooth. This allowed him the luxury of being whoever he wanted to be. Most of the time he convinced doctors that it was an inherited trait, so he wouldn't have to succumb to testing or questions; police officers were a different story. Their dominant personalities made tapping into their minds a bit of a challenge. He removed his hands from the loose zip straps, placed his fingertips on the glass, and watched the neon light move under the glass; no warmth seemed to pass his hand.

Alex looked up into the expectant eyes of the burly officer. He tapped into the mind of the officer. He realized that the confusion stemmed from the blank screen in front of the officer. The software did not find any prints and didn't perform a search. *Lex Macedo.* He sent the suggestion over to the officer. "Lex Macedo," the burly officer repeated as if under a spell, "let's get you processed."

He nodded to two officers who walked into the room.

Alex turned, and with a gracious smile, handed the remnants of the zip straps to the frowning task force leader. With a quick nod to Ed, he took a deep breath and walked with a casual air through the green double doors that would seal him from his freedom for an indefinite amount of time; then again time was on his side.

The hallway was sterile and devoid of any warmth. It opened up into a room which looked more like an unintended blister, rather than a room designed with a purpose.

Alex felt a rough shove towards the white wall with lines on it, which would serve to demarcate his height in the picture. *Ah, this must be for my mug shot.* He mused. *I wonder how that will come out. I have never taken a mug shot while I am imaging as someone else.*

"Stand in the feet."

Alex looked at the floor. A mat, like he had seen at airports, housed two orange blobs that bore little semblance to feet. He complied, placing his feet within the orange markers.

"Face front."

The flash blinded Alex as he turned right then left for the profile shots and stood waiting for further direction. One of the officers approached him holding a bin and the largest Ziploc plastic bag he'd ever seen.

"Remove your clothing down to your drawers. Put your accessories, change, etcetera in the bag and clothes in that there bin."

Alex stared at the man who had a thick southern drawl. "You're actually from Florida aren't you?"

"Son, if I were you, I'd keep your eyes focused on the task at hand. I'm not here to keep you company."

Alex smiled. "Fair enough, yes, sir." He removed his clothing and shoes. As directed, he took off his watch, bracelet, removed a large fold of money from his pocket and deposited all in the Ziploc bag.

"You can always tell the rich by their underwear."

"Ain't that right."

"Yeah, you get the wannabes that dress like they got it, but underneath they're wearing Fruit of the Loom just like everyone else."

"True enough. What brand do you think they are?"

"I don't know. All I know is they better drop like the regular ones, or that guy has got a problem."

Alex squinted his eyes at the officers. He looked down at his form fitting boxer briefs, not understanding what the fuss was about, why he had to remove them, and yet, glad that he had worn them. Underwear was not always a requirement for him.

"That's right, son, drop 'em and spread your cheeks."

Alex stared at the Floridian officer, the request not sinking in, "I'm sorry, I don't think I understand what you're asking of me."

"You speak English, this shouldn't be a problem. Pull down your underwears and spread your butt cheeks, I need to make sure you aren't smuggling money or drugs."

"And how do you plan on accomplishing that task?" Alex was quite indignant.

"I'm gonna shine a flashlight up your ass, son."

Alex stared deep into his eyes, "I just gave you a billfold of ten thousand dollars. I am neither smuggling money nor anything else for that matter." Lowering his voice so his vampiric powers of persuasion would be more than just a suggestion, he sent a mental blast to the officer. *I am not smuggling anything. Go join your cohort and figure out why the pictures haven't come out right.*

Satisfied with the dazed look that flooded into the Floridian officer's face, Alex stood with his arms folded waiting for his next obstacle. He watched the officer spin the flashlight around his finger before clipping it back on his belt. He threw an orange uniform at him. "Put that on."

The other officer thumped on the machine. "The damned machine just broke, check out this picture."

Alex tapped into the minds of the officers and saw they were looking at what appeared to be pictures within pictures of a man, or several men, with piercing bright lights for eyes. He smiled, zippering the uniform closed in a purposeful fashion he hoped would catch their attention. The sun was almost up, and he had yet to see what his sleeping quarters looked like.

Take me back to holding. Alex shot both men a persuasive blast.

"Take him back there, put him in the felon pen. We'll figure out what to do about his mug shot later."

"We still got have him sign for his stuff. Why the felon pen?" the Floridian asked.

"Well, he's not in for a misdemeanor and we'll get the stuff later."

"True enough. Hope he survives the night."

Alex felt the officer's hand on his arm; he could see he was reaching for the hand cuffs. *You don't need those, friend. I'll accompany you with no resistance.* Alex whispered, his voice laced with persuasion.

The officer pocketed the handcuffs and began down the hallway. They made a right and then a sharp left. Alex smiled with relief; they were heading into the center of the building with many floors above them. There was no chance that sunlight would be making an appearance in the holding cell. The sunlight wouldn't kill him at his age; it would deplete his strength which he was trying to conserve given the amount of unknown variables ahead of him.

The officer scanned his badge; a tiny high-pitched bleeping noise granted them entry. When the doors opened, Alex was unsure whether the doors had been sealed to keep the potential inmates in, or the smell. Foul scents offended his well-developed olfactory bulb. The stench of human decay and excrement overwhelmed him. The jangle of keys brought his focus back to the officer, who slid a key into the keyhole in the holding cell and slid the door back.

Shaking his head, Alex stepped inside. He heard the grate of metal against metal sealing his fate for the next few days. The holding pen, as it had been referred to, hosted about twenty potential inmates awaiting trial before being sent prison. They had backed up to the rear of the pen when the door slid open. After the clang of metal resounded and the officer had vacated the vicinity, they edged forward.

Alex scanned the unruly bunch. Some were murderers, thieves, with a couple being in for gang related crimes. He was able to make a quick assessment of leadership with his scan. An edge of fear hung in the air feeding his inner beast. A smile played at the corner of his mouth. Glancing upwards, Alex noted the position of the camera and gauged the frequency of its sweep.

"What the fuck are you laughing at motherfucker?"

"Save the attempt at dominance," Alex warned the approaching Cuban gang member, while still timing the camera's sweep. Not one inch of visible skin was without a tattoo. Some of them looked as if they were there to fill up space. The tattoos did not appear to be as beautiful or symbolic as those worn by the Yakusa; these were quite random in appearance. Even the Celtics had a tribal theme going on for them with their full body tattoos.

"Man, do you know who the fuck you're talking to?" The tattooed Latino raised his hands in an open invitation to brawl.

A low growl emanated from Alex's lips. He waited until the camera finished its sweep and sprang.

Chapter Four

Headlines flooded the six panels above Max's desk; his fingers were a blur as they flew over the keyboard with the speed of lightning. Leaning back into his computer chair, he paused to survey the information he retrieved.

"Shit, the news is all out," Max yelled into the living room. He scanned the monitors until he was joined by Jack, Miguel, Lina, and Leonidas.

"Look at that headline: Money Laundering scandal uncovered —Lex Macedo web-hosting billionaire has been arrested as a prime suspect. Look at this other one, Macedo Ink suspect as a front for counterfeit ring. CEO Lex Macedo arrested on charges of money laundering. Or even this one—Billionaire Lex

Macedo Arrested—they even have a picture of him in an orange jumpsuit."

"That has to be an inside job," Jack mused. "Someone is either trying to get rich with a quick sale of a picture, or someone on the inside is working for the enemy."

"Outside of me sucking the blood out of everyone down there, how do we find out and get to the bottom of this?" Lina turned to Jack.

"Follow the money trail. There has to be a source listed or a source paid."

"I'll start hacking into computers and see what I can find," Max offered. "What about the other money?"

"What other money?" Jack asked?

"Dad's money."

"No one can touch that right now," Leonidas held up his hand, "Macedo Ink operational funds are still available. Alexander Macedo's funds are still available, as are a few of his other aliases. The only real funds that have been frozen are Lex's and the shell companies that we use to hold certain other funds."

"How did this happen, Leo?" Lina asked.

Max watched Leonidas' hands as he tossed them in the air in what seemed like despair. The ancient vampire sighed, leaving Max to wonder if he wasn't hiding something.

"I noticed about a year ago that a few unusual things started occurring. When I say unusual, I mean they initiated an awareness which I have learned to take note of." Leonidas ran his hand over his hair.

"Like what?" Max asked.

"Like a woman riding down my street at the very same time every day and she didn't live within a twenty-mile radius from my house."

"How would you know that?" Max squinted his left eye showing his curiosity.

"You are not the only one with facial recognition software, my son." Leonidas laughed.

"Gotcha."

"Then my neighbors changed and all of a sudden I started getting their mail. They would pop over to retrieve it."

"Apart from the woman on the bike, you do know that all sounds kinda normal, right?" Jack stated. "And even then, the woman could have been checking out the neighborhood before deciding on buying her dream home."

"These neighbors have been married to each other for forty years, lived and maintained the same routine for forty years. I do not believe that people so satisfied with their lives would make such a change so readily. So I became suspect; hence, I moved. While they slept, I had the whole house packed up and vacated. My mail was collected from the post office daily, and I was kind enough to place a forwarding address from my home to theirs for the intruders. I tracked down that they purposefully used my address prior to moving so I left the surveillance system intact. It only took a week before they got curious enough to climb the fence and break into the house. They walked around checking the walls and floors. I called a police friend and had them arrested. He called me later to tell me that they were agents of the FATF."

"Wow," Jack mused, "all of that from awareness."

"Things got quiet for a while because they couldn't figure out where I had gone, but I had a need to surface in Florida and as soon as I did they were on me."

"Which means they have a list of our safe houses," Max ruminated reaching for his glass of A+, "the vampire council needs to be alerted."

"I have not been able to send word, as I suspected that my information was being tapped. I encrypted all of my files and sent them to the cloud in an upstream under the pretense of a download of music."

"They'll probably be making arrangements for a visit after seeing these headlines," Lina muttered.

"So what now?" Max grumbled, not quite ready to see what even a segment of the vampire council looked like. He recalled stories he overheard his father and Augy, a master vampire and his closest friend, talking about. It all seemed so surreal and a little overwhelming.

"I think we've formed a tentative plan for now," Jack smiled,

"I think we just work our plan until we figure it all out or need to change it. Max, you figure out who took and sold the picture of Lex and check on the safety of those files in the cloud. Lina, you are going to go down to Florida and talk to Alex. By the time you get there, they should be talking about bail. We should try to get him out of jail before he is sent to prison to await trial. Life will get extremely challenging for him if he gets sent to The Wing."

"The Wing?" Max asked.

"Hmmm, I thought everyone has heard of it. I guess maybe only those who are in law enforcement would know about it. The Wing is about the worst holding facility in the nation. They are overcrowded and under manned. Miguel, I'm thinking you should go with Lina; she's not going to be able to do any recon when she gets there. I'm sure the press will be all over Alex. It's possible that no one will let him out of their sight. We have to be able to get some decent Intel while down there."

"I don't think that's a good idea," Miguel started.

"Why not!" Jack interjected.

"You'd be left vulnerable."

"I would be honored to stand and fight," Leonidas bowed.

"I'm here too," Max laughed, "If that's any consolation." Even as a vampire, Max knew that no one thought of him as a fighter. One day he'd have to learn; for now he'd rather focus on getting over the thirst so he could be with Sam.

"I'll go down twenty-four hours before Lina gets there and see what I can find out. There should be no difference in available information between the time that I go and Lina, rather, Alex's image gets there."

"Thank you, Miguel."

Max watched as Jack grinned like a Cheshire cat rushing forward to reward Miguel's concession with a kiss. He missed the days where he could hold Sam without worry that he'd hurt her. He watched Miguel run his fingers through Jack's hair and realized how much he missed Sam's head of thick, untamed curls that poked him in the face as they slept. They smelled of vanilla candle wax, citrus oils, and Mediterranean spices.

Finding himself alone in his office after everyone dispersed to take care of their tasks, Max ran his tongue over the retainer. He played with it while thinking of his need to be with Sam. He would conquer the insatiable thirst, just as sure as he would make sure his dad got home safe and sound.

With his resolve set, he spun around in his captain's chair and reached for another deep swig of A+ before returning to his new focus; finding an inconspicuous entrance into the newspapers' mainframe. He had to find the leaky source.

CHAPTER FIVE

The sun was almost up; Lina could feel the night submit to the dawning intensity of the day. A smile played across her face as she felt Archimedes become lax on her shoulder. Her hand instinctively cradled his head. She walked towards the crib and laid him gently on the soft navy cotton sheets. The crib was decorated in bold colors. It had none of the pastels and floating animals that could usually be found in a baby's crib.

"You are such a little vampire. Awww, you take after your Papi." Lina chuckled, patting Archimedes on the head. "He'll be home soon my darling, and we'll be a family again." At the same time, a fear resided deep within her over her son's vulnerability.

She stared at his fair complexion and dark features. His

brown curly hair sat like a crown atop his head. He already had the promise of thick illustrious eyebrows, a prominent nose, and pouting lips. Lina remembered the first time she had commented on the handsomeness of her son. "Oh Archimedes, I hope your Papi is okay. Remember when I told you that you would be a 'Lady Killer' and your Papi said, "Not if I can help it." He was so serious, but he was right. While you will become a devilishly handsome hybrid, half vampire and half demon, you will have to learn to use your powers with wisdom, just like your Papi." Lina held onto the memory as she tucked Archimedes in. The memory became so powerful, she could almost feel Alex's hands encircle her waist, and the smell of his essence assaulted her senses. She stood up straight finding her will power, "I promise this to you, son; I will bring Papi home."

A knock at the door caught her attention, "Come in." Lina stood poised with one hand placed in the other.

Jesus, the hell hound, entered first inhaling deeply, looking around the room as he padded over to Lina. He rubbed his giant head against her and flopped on the floor. Lina cocked her head as tiny fingers rounded the door. "Come on in, Mirella."

A childlike head followed the fingers. At a quick glance, Mirella could be mistaken for a child based on her stature, but when she smiled, the permanent fangs displayed would be the second give away, the first being her eyes. They were completely green and unchanging. Mirella was a wood nymph. Vines grew up the walls as she entered the room. Lina watched as her wings flitted, making a low humming sound.

"Thank you for coming on such short notice," Lina smiled.

"Is he asleep?"

"He is," Lina pointed at the crib, "I don't expect him to wake until tonight."

"Will you return by the eve?"

"I'm not sure; I have to check on Alexander. Once I know he is okay and we have eliminated our threat then you can return home."

"How is Alexander?"

"I will find out before day's end." Lina forced a smile.

"Who can I trust?"

"The list is short: Miguel, the Warrior of Light; Jacqui Brunson, the Peace Keeper for Terra; and Max Macedo, son of Alexander."

"I smell another upstairs."

"You have the list for now. Time is too young to make exceptions. Jesus will help you." Lina looked at her hell hound with favor; he picked up his head grinning like a normal bully-dog. "The refrigerator is fully stocked. If anything, you know how to get in touch with me."

"Yes, ma'am," Mirella smiled.

"Very well," Lina walked out of her bedroom giving a longing look at the crib where her sleeping child lay. She chuckled, seeing the child-like figure of Mirella wave then rested a hand on Jesus' head. If a human had seen her leave her baby in the hands of a child and a dog, some agency would be knocking on her door within seconds. But the two guarding her baby were two of the most lethal creatures currently standing in Terra. Lina sighed.

Standing in her living room, she focused on the job at hand.

Okay, I need to get to Florida as Alejandro. What do I need? A plane? We have one of those. How am I going to sustain that image? Ah, I need my dress. Crap! I don't think it's with my other dresses. I need my dress made from the skin of the red wolf. Wolves after all are the ultimate shape changers.

Lina tapped her forehead with her finger before tapping a rift and landing in her room on the sixth level of hell. The torches breathed fire the moment her room recognized her presence. She walked to her closet and thumbed through her dresses. Dragon-skin, Leviathon, Demon-skin—A change in the air caused her to spin around with fangs bared.

She hissed her displeasure at seeing her father standing before her.

"Now, now," Lucifer waggled his finger. "Is that any way at all to greet your dear old father?"

"If this is the same father that tried to set me up and then kill me and my unborn child? Then yes!" Lina hissed, eyeing him warily. She could tell that he hadn't recovered to his full strength, but he was never a character to be underestimated; ever.

"Tsk, tsk, tsk, my dear. That is the past. This is the now. I've seen the error of my ways… yada, yada, yada. Won't you forgive your old man?" Lucifer waved his hand in a circular motion to mean, and so on and so forth. "I want to make amends."

"Why?" Lina placed her hands on her hips. She couldn't trust him.

"I want to see my grandson."

"I'm still not feeling so warm and fuzzy Daddy darling." Lina cooed watching him frown at the hated expression.

"What are you looking for?"

"My red dress."

"You have plenty of red dresses."

"I'm looking for the one given to me by the red wolf."

"Given?" Lucifer raised an eyebrow, "that's a bit of a stretch."

"Do you know where it is or not?"

"Didn't you leave it with that wolf? What's his name? Bane?" Lucifer raised his left brow. "As in he was the bane of my existence while you were with him."

"Lane," Lina exhaled, as a pang of desire jolted through her. Lane had been quite a lust interest in his day. "How did you remember him? That has to be over a century ago?"

"There was always something about that black wolf that rubbed me the wrong way."

"Everybody who doesn't succumb to your wishes rubs you the wrong way," Lina walked up to him and planted a kiss on his forehead, "thank you Daddy. I have to change."

She whirled around in a swish of fabric; the air changed, signifying her father's exit. Peeling off the night's clothes, she put on something she knew Lane would appreciate. Reaching into the depths of her closet, she found the corset and garter belt that he had purchased for her. With breasts a little fuller and hips a tad wider since childbirth, Lina decided she much preferred her new body. Especially after a good squeeze into the black and red lace number. She donned a night gown made of Chinese Dragon Breath. It covered her like the dusk's shadows, leaving much to the imagination and more to hunger for.

She tapped into a rift and landed on a ledge on the face of the Apennine mountain range just outside the mouth of a cavern.

It was difficult to walk in heels on the uneven ground. Lina decided to take them off, as they made her appear unsure and lacking in confidence. Six eyes blinked at her from the shadows and a low growl rumbled at her.

"Where's Lane?" Lina growled in return, her incisors dropping ready for a fight.

One of the wolves nodded into the depths of the cavern. She followed behind the one, acutely aware of the two other wolves that followed behind her. They kept to the shadows, but their stealth was no match for her awareness.

The cavern opened up onto a large area lit by the filtered rays of the moon through a crack in the side of the mountain face.

Lina scanned the room; an old man sat on one of the flat rocks that were positioned side by side. Piercing yellow eyes regarded her from under the scarcely peppered snow white hair, which fell past his shoulders. *Thrones—and if so then his Alpha bitch is not here right now.*

"Lane." Lina smiled.

The old man got up. "Time has been kind to you."

Lina smiled again pressing her lips into Lane's velvety, sun-kissed cheek, "And not to you. How long has it been?"

"At least one hundred years, Catalina De Diablo. To what do I owe this visit?" Lane stepped back.

Lina could feel the weight of his gaze still upon her. She adjusted her gown; it fell open to display her assets. "You have something of mine?"

"And what is that, my dear?" Lane moved forward. "There was a time that I waited to hear those exact words leave your lips."

Lina felt his hands slide underneath the opening of her gown in a familiar fashion. He ran his thumbs over the crest of each ripe bosom. She was shocked that her body still responded to him. While his appearances might be that of an old man, Lina knew nothing was wrong with his agility, gauging from the way he hopped off his throne. Something about him still struck her as hot and sexy, but he was no Alex. Even in his youth, he did not compare to Alex. She resisted the urge to shiver. Running her hands along his long, lean body, she recognized that his skin and muscles were still firm. Only the white of his shoulder length hair betrayed his age. She pressed her lips against his ear, allowing an incisor to scrape the skin as she spoke, "I want my dress."

A low rumble ran up Lane's chest, "I don't know my love, I rather prefer you out of your clothes."

Lina felt the ribbons lacing up the corset become slack, her breasts threatened to spill over the demi cups. Images of Alex flooded her mind. Closing her eyes, she bared all four of her fangs and smiled. *I am not betraying Alejandro; I must do what I must do to help him.* She nuzzled in Lane's neck, "You may have what you want, but I need my dress back." Lina pressed up against the old black wolf in his human form, moving him backwards in a synchronized dance until he sat down on the flat rock resembling a throne. She arched her neck. He nuzzled her skin and inhaled her essence. She straddled his legs, evoking a moan of desire from him. "So what do you want Lane?"

"What the fuck is going on?" An angry growl echoed around the cavern.

Lina inhaled the new scents. Spinning around, she faced the angry challenge. The Alpha bitch had returned with the rest of the pack.

Lane jumped up. Anticipating his response, Lina deftly side-stepped so as not to be thrown to the ground. She closed her gown around her eyeing up the new Alpha bitch. *Black hair, blue eyes. Oh, so northern Italian and what a temper. She is young too. Lane always did like youth.* Lina alternated her gaze between Lane and his Alpha mate. A pang hit her. *I am not jealous. I am not jealous. What I have with Alejandro is much more than what I had with Lane. Lane was… well he just was. It was fun, but Alejandro is so much more than that. Perhaps Lane has found what I couldn't give him in her.* Lina sighed. *I suppose I can't blame the bitch for getting her hackles in a twist. Let's just hope she doesn't challenge me so I don't have to kill her. I would hate for Lane to be alone again. He's so delicious, he deserves more than that.*

"Back down Danika, this is unfinished business." Lane growled.

"Like hell it is. Looks as if you were ready to start new business." The She-wolf bared her teeth.

Lina eyed her up, "No need to get territorial. I have not asserted any claim."

Danika turned to Lane, "What the fuck is that supposed to mean?"

Lina felt Lane's glare, but shrugged her shoulders in nonchalance until she felt a jacket being thrown at her feet. From medieval times to date, the significance of articles of clothing thrown at another have always meant, the fight was on.

Looking up from the jacket, Lina met Lane's pleading eyes. She walked around the jacket allowing her gown to traipse after her making sure that nothing touched the jacket. "Lane, we still have a matter to discuss. I told you I would give you whatever you want in return for my dress. To be clear, I would never intend to lose a fight; though I might be disinclined to acknowledge the challenge, for old times."

Lane looked at his Alpha female and sighed, "Danika, this is a fight that you could never recover from. This is Catalina De Diablo, the original Alpha of this clan. She fought alongside me and killed the Red wolf. The skin that gives this clan its powers is hers. The dress that hangs in the vault was fashioned for her alone. No one can wield its power, except for her. It is because I love you, that I cannot deny her its return."

Lane scaled the rocks to the rear of the cavern with the agility of youth, and pressed a hidden button. The rock face jutted outwards and slid to the left. Lina watched as Lane disappeared. She glanced at Danika, who still had her lips curled in a permanent growl. Lina shook her head in disgust, uncontrollable anger was so ugly. She made a mental note to remind herself of that fact.

The entire pack crouched when Lane returned with the dress. The rock face slid back into place and Lane made his way back down towards Lina. He stopped right in front of her with a breath's space between them. Lina felt the dress pressed into her hands.

"Lane, I didn't mean to kick up such a fuss between you and

your lady wolf. I was just reminiscing for old times." Lina looked down at the dress now secure in her grasp. Lane hung his head. It rested just above hers. His breath was hot against her temple

"The old times were great, but times have changed."

"Indeed."

"Lina, my pack will be vulnerable without this dress."

"My need is great; I have not come to collect on a mere whim. I will make a promise to you. A promise not to be taken lightly. I will return it to you for safe keeping when I have satisfied my need." Lina looked up and kissed Lane on his chin, "Stay safe, Lane."

Lina didn't wait until she was outside to tap the rift. Once the dress was within her clutches she took two steps backwards and was gone.

The rift opened up in the community kitchen. She began pacing.

"Everything okay?"

Lina spun around. "Jack, I didn't hear you. Either you have become proficient at stealth—"

"Or, you were really preoccupied." Jack laughed. "You look as if something is bothering you."

"Yes. No. I don't know," Lina walked over to the nearest bar stool that hugged the large island and sat in it still clutching the red dress.

"Nice dress."

"Don't touch it," Lina snapped, clutching the dress tighter.

Jack raised her hands as she stepped onto the bar stool across from Lina.

"I didn't mean it like that, well I did, but not so mean," Lina chuckled, "The dress has powers that could hurt you. You're not a wolf, so it is probably best that you didn't touch it."

"Yeah, I'm pretty wary of you and a red dress," Jack laughed back at her, "they don't use red for warning for no good reason. Is the dress the source of your issues?"

"Yes and no," Lina scratched her head, "I had to go and ask an old acquaintance for it. I left it with him. As a matter of fact, I left in rather a hurry. Lane, the black wolf and I were kinda serious back then and it seemed that he wanted to settle down; I wasn't ready. So I bolted," Lina looked at Jack, "You know what I mean, right?"

Satisfied that Jack nodded, Lina went on. "So when I went back there today, it was as if he wanted to pick up right where we left off. Granted, I wasn't much help because I was dressed like this," Lina pulled her gown to the side to display her corset ensemble.

"Wow that's a serious getup," Jack gasped, "umm, is your night gown going to eat me, too?"

Lina checked her gown. The corner was trying to crawl up Jack's leg. She pulled it back, "No you're fine."

"It felt creepy, but go on," Jack urged.

"It's just that when things started getting all thick and heavy, all I could think about was Alejandro. Lane is a hot guy and terribly sexy, but he is not Alejandro in any way."

Jack smiled, "You really love him, don't you?"

"Alejandro?" Lina hung her head, "It is a weakness."

"It is your strength," Jack smiled, "Love. Real love can move mountains and conquer cities. Don't think of it like a human emotion; just take it for what it is. You love your husband and would do anything for him."

"So you don't think I'm weak?" Lina mused.

"You got the dress."

"Only because the Alpha female returned and Lane chose her life."

"Did he choose her life because he loved her, or because he would rather look weak in front of his pack?"

"Hmmm, Jack the Peace Keeper of Terra; I will think on this love business," Lina laughed, "I have a date with my husband." Lina peeled off her Dragon-breath gown and passed it to Jack.

"Oh shit Lina, this feels cold and icky." Jack whined.

"Take it upstairs to Max. Ask him to hang it up, the gown prefers to float."

Lina pulled on the skin of the red wolf. She felt the power wash over her like the g-force from a thirty second roller coaster ride. It felt exhilarating every time. Watching Jack scurry towards the elevator she called to her, "Thanks Jack for the talk, it helped."

Jack turned.

Lina watched the confusion and amazement flood into her face.

"Alex? Lina? Holy shit Lina, is that you?"

"Yeah, it's me."

"Fuck that's creepy. What are you going to do about your voice? You look like Alex, but your voice, it still sounds like you."

Lina laughed as Jack still held the shadow gown away from her body like it was a disease.

"Stop laughing at me." Jack scowled.

"I need to hear his voice, so I can replicate it," Lina laughed, "otherwise this is going to be a silent movie."

"Ummm, let's call his cell phone. It should go straight to voice mail. Or just do that mental thing that you guys do."

"Good idea on using voicemail. His voice doesn't sound the same in my head as it does out loud."

Jack fished her cell phone out and swiped her password on the touch screen. "Call Alex," she spoke into the phone putting it on speaker phone.

Lina listened to the phone ringing half hoping that he would pick up, and the whole jail thing would just be someone's idea of a rotten joke. The voice mail kicked in and Alex's deep rumble filtered across the frame relay to the tiny speaker. She focused on his voice picking up his timbre and cadence.

After a moment, Lina repeated the message. "Thanks for calling. I'm not here. You know what to do. I'll call you back."

Jack took two steps back, "That's almost scary."

"Scary bad, scary good?" Lina switched back to her own voice.

"You sounded just like him."

"Then I'm ready," she smiled.

CHAPTER SIX

The holding pen could have held pigs based on the squalid conditions. One metal seat-less toilet rose out of the ground like a festering pimple. Urine and feces leaked out of the toilet bowl dripping on to the floor. The pooled sludge made a single riveted line to the drain in the middle of the holding pen.

Miguel landed on the corner of the cage finding the division amongst the felons quite amusing. Alexander lay on the bench with his hands folded across his chest on one side of the pen, while all nineteen felons stood with fear written across their faces on the other.

"Even in this stench riddled cage, I smell you."

Miguel froze time.

"I would think that with the stench that you would welcome such a pleasant scent?" Miguel materialized in the cage by the door, furthest from the defecation.

Alex swung his legs over the end of the bench and stood up, "Brother, you are indeed a welcome sight."

"Lina is on her way down," Miguel smiled, patting Alex on the back. He released him after seeing him in his true form, "Take advantage of the brief moment of frozen time to gather your energies."

"I have found ways to draw from the humans without hurting them. I should be okay; though I do relish this short time as myself. Lina is coming here?"

"Yes, though not as Lina," Miguel chuckled, "as you."

"As me, how is she going to maintain—"

"I'm guessing that you are familiar with the dress fashioned from the skin of the Red Wolf." Miguel cocked his head to read Alex. For a brief moment, he could have sworn he sensed, or saw a flicker of sadness.

"I am; she left it in the keeping of the Black Wolf." Alex muttered.

"But you are troubled by this?"

"Not in the whole scheme of things."

"Something did seem to upset you, though."

"They were an Alpha pair many eons ago."

"Ah, well I wouldn't worry. Your wife would do anything for

you."

"That is the part that troubles me," Alex sat on the bench staring at the frozen expressions of the felons across from him, "tell me about what you know."

Miguel frowned, "Not much, yet. The headlines are out, which is why it made sense for Alexander Macedo to come down to bail out his brother. Leonidas showed up at the tower with some information which Max thinks is safe. Although I have a feeling Max doesn't trust Leonidas and I'm on the fence, as they say. Someone on the inside leaked a picture of Lex in an orange jumpsuit, and I'm here to find out who on the inside here is on the take. I just thought I'd stop by to say hello, and see if you had any ideas."

"If you can find that blasted task force leader or Ed Trattoria, start with them." Alex mumbled.

"Oh, before I forget," Miguel reached into his inner suit pocket and withdrew a bag of blood. He handed it to Alex.

"The beautiful thing about you angels," Alex mumbled before he sunk his teeth into the bag of blood, "is that you are so damn warm. This almost feels real if it weren't for the tinges of anticoagulant."

"You're welcome." Miguel laughed, taking the drained bag back. "We'll make regular visits then just in case a bag is better that your misting method."

"Sounds good."

Miguel watched as Alex lay back down on the bench. As he dematerialized, he released time.

"Were you talking to me?" one of the felons asked.

Miguel chuckled as Alex turned his head as Lex Macedo to bare his teeth in a growl, drawing gasps from the felons.

He walked through the double doors, paused at an intersection and cocked his head in the direction of distant voices then followed the path through sterile corridors adorned with occasional legal notices.

Inhaling, Miguel recognized a familiar scent. He honed in on it dematerializing through walls to stand behind Ed Trattoria, who sat with another officer around a long table with a white board with names and photographs pinned to it in a conference room. Papers lay strewn across the table. It was clear that this pair hadn't slept for a while.

"Dude, you still don't look much better."

The black Kevlar reinforced uniform, outfitted with all types of weaponry, made Miguel wonder if the speaker lounging with his feet on the conference table wasn't the task force leader. He sent Alex a mental image for confirmation.

"I'll be fine," Trattoria laughed, "you think a little Florida sun is going to get me down. I've been after something on one of these guys for a while now. I'm not letting go of this break."

"How did you get this information again? Don't you think it's odd that our investigation just crashed into a perfect fit?"

Ed sighed, "No, it just means we each have good Intel."

"Or we are being fed information."

"I'd prefer not to second guess good fortune."

"We'll see how reliable it is. It has to stand up in court. That's the bottom line."

"Did you ever get that judge to add Macedo to the warrant?" Ed coughed.

"No, but not to worry. I know the prosecutor who knows the judge. It'll be covered."

"You sound sure of yourself," Ed smiled.

Their conversation faded into the background as Miguel visually rummaged through the paperwork on the table. He sniffed Ed's folder trying to filter Trattoria's greasy scent. Exhaling quickly, he isolated a scent. Every entity had its own trace scent. "Soucouyant!"

Looking at the white board, he scanned the scribbling of names and events under pictures. An artist's drawing caught his eye. A beautiful black woman with beguiling eyes leapt from the white page. Neat dreadlocks framed her face, which featured a wide flat nose and voluptuous pillow lips.

Miguel flipped his hand casually to freeze time in the room. He scanned the room for digital cameras. They sometimes caused a problem for him. Good fortune was in the stars. The room didn't have any cameras.

Reaching into his pocket, he took out his phone and snapped

pictures of the whiteboard, focusing on the dark beauty captured in the pencil drawing. Turning to the conference room table he snapped pictures of every piece of paper in and out of files.

Reanimating time, Miguel left the conference room and wandered down the hall to Judge Sander's office, where he heard heated voices. Dematerializing, he walked through the wall and sat in the chair in the judge's chambers. The chair was one of two in front of the ominous mahogany desk. Trimmed with nail heads, turned wooden arms, and tufted Corinthian leather on the ladder back; this chair was old, worn, and quite comfortable. Miguel settled in; crossing his legs.

"How long do you expect no one to notice that this man has slipped through the cracks?" The Judge asked, as she flipped through the pages pinned in the folder in front of her.

"If you would just sign the warrant adding his name," the prosecutor pleaded.

"You haven't given me enough reason," Judge Sanders continued, "this folder that you say mysteriously appeared in New York is not acceptable. Can we validate it? Find me the person who provided it. Anonymous doesn't hold water with me. I need to understand their level of involvement. Has the FATF confirmed that these companies are actually laundering money? Where are the confirmed results of their investigation?"

"C'mon Judge, he'll be extradited."

"Rami, then let him be extradited. Why do we want this

here?"

"This could be good press for us."

"This man has money to hire the best lawyers in history. This was not a clean drill. I don't need that kind of floodlight on this judicial system, especially when there have been so many abysses he has been pushed into and through." Judge Sanders folded the folder, "I'll give you until the bail hearing. If you still have nothing by that time, I'll set bail so he can release himself."

"Yes, Judge," the prosecutor shook his head.

"It's the best I can do. Tell the police force to get their shit in gear!"

"It's the FATF Judge, along with a New York Detective."

"Better yet, international is even more reason to keep the light off us. Have him tried elsewhere." Judge Sanders handed the folder back to the prosecutor, who rose to take it from her.

Miguel noted a single bead of sweat beginning a path of descent as it trickled down his forehead. He jumped out the chair and followed him into the hallway, where he watched the man pull his cell phone out of his pocket and dialed a number. He was a full head shorter than Miguel, giving him the advantage of height. He looked at the touchscreen as the numbers were punched in seeing the smartphone resolve the number to display a single word, 'Chen.'

"Chinese," Miguel whispered, stepping back as the prosecutor turned around with vigor. He kept close to the man to hear the other end of the conversation.

"Hello," the prosecutor rubbed his forehead to rid the bead of sweat.

Miguel heard the thick Chinese accent from the incoming voice; he couldn't understand it. He noted the time, twenty-one minutes after eight in the morning. Maybe Max could trace the call once he figured out who the prosecutor was.

"I think we might have a problem," the prosecutor looked around, "no, nothing like that, just that the Judge is refusing to sign the warrant to add Macedo's name—no, no, please don't. I'll take care of it myself. Everything will go as planned. I promise."

Miguel knit his brows as the prosecutor ended the call and sank against the cold wall of the hallway. Moments passed before he pushed himself off and walked with purpose down the hallway taking left and right turns. Miguel lengthened his stride to keep up with him. For a short man, he sure walked at a good clip.

He stopped outside an inconspicuous door and inserted a key. It could have been a storage closet if it weren't for the name plate on the door. "Ramiro Santiago—Rami, you have been identified." Miguel found himself standing alone in the hallway with the door moments before his face. The prosecutor had gone inside. Pursing his lips, he walked through the door to find a small room lined with shelving units. Each shelf held boxes upon boxes of files. Some with lids off and others with files laid on top of them.

Miguel ducked to peer through the space between the files and the next shelf. As he did so an explosion sounded and a wet substance hit his face. Standing up, he depressed a firm finger into his cheek and wiped the substance off. Frowning, he inspected the red thickening substance, "Brain matter, great."

Side stepping the shelving unit, he saw Prosecutor Ramiro Santiago slumped backwards over his desk. He had fallen with his arms spread outward, the gun still entangled in his finger.

"I think that's enough reconnaissance for today," Miguel grit his teeth and dematerialized.

CHAPTER SEVEN

"Any statements, Mr. Macedo?...

"Is your brother the head of a money laundering ring, Mr. Macedo?"

Multiple voices uttered the same foundation questions, each stumbling over the other. The reporters were packed like sardines into a tiny space vying for the coveted spotlight and attention. Cameras flashed white, brilliant, blinding light. Lina shielded her eyes concentrating on imaging her husband, Alexander Macedo.

Microphones were pressed into her path as she moved forward from the limousine, up the steps of the Gilford Justice building. She mumbled a gruff, "No comment," and kept moving forward. She had secured a lawyer for the bail hearing and gave him a quick rundown of what was expected. The lawyer, walking at her side, pointed up the stairs; she nodded and closed the distance between them. Lina adjusted Alex's shades and glanced upward. She pursed her lips when she saw Miguel standing at the top of the stairs.

"Any news?" Lina stuck her hands in the suit pocket to refrain from touching Miguel and instead allowed him to touch her as he would have Alex. Feminine habits were difficult to break.

"I'd say." Miguel looked around.

"How is he?" Lina hoped her voice didn't betray her emotions.

"I've seen wild animals kept in better conditions."

"Hmmm, direction?"

"Perhaps a debriefing after the hearing would be best," Miguel whispered, "curious twists have unfolded."

Entering the justice building held its challenges. The digital equipment didn't see Alexander Macedo, it saw the shape of Lina as she walked through. Her skeletal system was quite different from the average human. Lina was thankful that Miguel was there to help persuade the officers to see what they wanted them to see.

"Thanks, Mig, I'm not sure that I would have gotten through all of that if you weren't here," Lina whispered.

Miguel smiled.

"Mr. Macedo, this way, please," the lawyer beckoned.

The lawyer stood at the escalator. Lina followed him up the moving stairway, remembering that she shouldn't grip onto Miguel for support. They rounded the corner of the escalator and entered Judge Sander's courtroom.

Rows of pew-like seating lined the rear of the courtroom, separated by a walkway, which concluded at a podium flanked by two basic tables and a number of chairs. Lina scanned the room noting that more chairs lined the right wall and a section cordoned off with chairs lined the left wall. She reached into her right suit pocket and withdrew her mobile phone depressing the volume down button until she felt it vibrate in her hand. Satisfied, she pocketed the device. The lawyer ushered her into the first pew on the right hand side.

"He'll be seated over there," Miguel pointed.

Lina followed the direction of his finger to the double row of chairs in the cordoned off section.

She nodded, crossing her legs.

Less ladylike, please.

Lina made a conscious effort to relax her legs as she looked around the lawyer, who almost blocked her view while he talked to the new prosecutor.

Alejandro, Amor how are you?

Well my Love, this is either the best decision I've ever made in my life, or the worst one ever.

You can stop this all right now.

But the threats will continue, I refuse to live my life looking over my shoulder. I want this over and done with.

Amor, so much of me just wants to blow this place up. We can start again, fresh. It's killing me to see you locked up like an animal.

It wouldn't be so terrible if I were just caged like an animal, these people suffer so much.

Papi, please…

Stay the course, Babe, this saga is exploding with an exponential factor and becoming bigger than I am rather quickly. I'm so pleased that you came down here as me. Excellent thinking. That factor alone will be confusing to the enemy and may draw them out even quicker, but we have to stay the course. Trust me, I question my decision at every turn, but I remember Max, Archimedes and you. I just don't want to have to look over our shoulders more than we have to. I would like him to grow up in a fairly normal life. However normal of a life, a hybrid child of the Prince of Abaddon and a Dark Warrior might have.

Lina sighed, *I agree. I just don't like Archimedes being without a father, or me being without a husband. I don't like being forced to be away from you.*

I love you too, babe. No matter what happens here we have to pull together to figure this out. You may want to talk to the Vampire Council.

They won't acknowledge me.

Take Leonidas with you. They'll concede. Talk to Ishtyn. Dammit! These are extenuating circumstances that may change the whole vampiric community's way of life. They need to understand the need for an exception and have a sense of urgency.

The sound of the gavel banging its wooden block brought Lina's focus back to the courtroom. She stood as requested when the judge brought the courtroom to session. She watched the judge and prosecutor scrutinizing their every move.

Amor, both the judge and prosecutor look clean.

I agree

They'll clear you.

No, they won't.

Why not?

Because I'm going to make sure they don't.

Lina jumped, as a blast of persuasion reverberated off the judge. She watched as she changed courses.

"Prosecutor Gaines, please switch to the Macedo case. What do we have?"

"Well, Judge, I've been reviewing this file all morning; we have nothing."

"Nothing?"

The lawyer Lina retained stood up and walked to the podium, "Judge, we asked for bail to be set at one hundred thousand dollars. My client has no arrest history whatsoever. He has been a steward of citizenship, donating to police and fire departments across the nation—"

"Based on the circumstances, bail is denied pending extradition."

Amor, why did you do that, they have nothing?

The whole thing has been a comedy of errors, and when I'm ready I'll be released on that fact alone. Until then, our real enemy is not them, and they are going to have to play their hand soon. They have no one left on the inside as I can make out. The prosecutor that should have been trying this case was Ramiro Santiago. Find out what they had on him. Talk to Miguel. I know he has something. There's a rumor going around that Santiago shot himself this morning.

Okay, Amor, if you need me, you know I'll tear the hearts out of anyone who dare torment you.

Thank you for protecting me and what I believe to be true even when you don't.

That's what partners do, right?

Right.

Lina patted Miguel on the knee, nodded to the lawyer motioning that they were leaving. As she walked down the walkway to the courtroom doors, she heard Alex calling her. Pausing before she left, she gave him one last look.

Yes, Amor?

If at all possible darling, do me one more favor

What's that?

Your walk.

What's wrong with my walk? I thought you liked my walk?

While you are masquerading as Alexander Macedo, could you try to walk a little more like me and a little less like you?

Lina smiled and walked out the door followed by Miguel.

I will try, Amor, I will try.

She walked to the limousine in silence. The further she walked from Alex, the deeper the void within her felt. She had lived for what felt like an eternity without him, and yet these few short years together made her only want the existence that had him in it. She mulled over the information he had given her and looked at Miguel without asking questions . Ears and eyes within the facility could be tracking their every move.

The reporters were still outside snapping their pictures. Lina wondered what the headlines would read this time. She was sure half the information was fabricated. She slowed her pace, wondering if she should leak some information to swing the ball in Alex's favor. No, he was correct, the timing was not right, yet. Picking back up the pace, she headed towards the car. She felt Miguel's hand at her shoulder in a manly fashion and wondered if he had picked up on her thoughts.

Once in the limousine with the doors secured, she depressed the call button.

"Yes, boss," the driver answered.

"The airfield please, and lock us down if you would," Lina used Alex's voice one last time.

The locks sounded around the limo. A dark, opaque screen closed off the driver from Lina and Miguel. She shook herself free of Alex's image, kicked off his shoes and crossed her legs.

"Feel better?" Miguel laughed.

"You have no idea," Lina grinned.

"I don't mean to stick my nose where it doesn't belong, but when this is all over you might want to put Alexander's mind at ease."

"In what way?"

"He seemed to have some feelings about the dress you're wearing."

"He didn't trust me?" Lina ran her fingers down the fine, soft pelt of the wolf-skin dress.

"I don't think that it amounted to that. I think he trusts you in every way to have his back and do what's necessary. I think the question often is, do we want what is necessary?"

Lina rubbed the dress, "I understand and thank you," her smile was momentary, "first I need to get him back." She flipped down the armrest between the seats and tapped the buttons on the wood grained console. The mechanical sounds of a projection screen lowering dominated the limousine.

Dialing could be heard as Lina punched more buttons, "Shit, I hope I did this right. Alex usually does this."

"I think you did something right," Miguel pointed to Max's face on the screen, "Hi, Max."

Lina looked up smiling into Max's grin, "Hey there, please make sure this line is secure before we begin. I've been punching buttons, but who knows what I've done."

"No problem," Max looked away.

Lina could hear his fingers flying over the keyboard. A golden lock at the top right hand corner of the screen caught her attention, "There we go, thanks Max."

"So how did it go?"

"Your Dad is adamant about seeing it through and in his way." Lina started.

"That may well be because a strange turn of events has started. I still don't know who is behind it all, although I'm beginning to feel as if we have a major player moving the chess pieces." Miguel reached into his pocket. "Is there a thingy to hook up to the phone to get these pictures to you, Max?"

"Is that a Macedo Ink phone?" Max asked.

"Yes?"

"Then it should just plug into the armrest."

Lina took the phone and turned it over to check the receptacle. Pushing a button on the armrest, a hidden cover opened revealing a connection for the phone to slide into.

"It's hooked up."

"Really, Miguel?"

"What?"

"There's like a hundred pictures of Jack here."

"I don't know how to get those off. Just scroll to the bottom and you'll find them," Miguel laughed, "I took pictures of information from the files and the white board. The one file smelled like a soucouyant, and there was a drawing of a beautiful, dark-skinned woman. I'm thinking that's her."

"Who?"

"I think that the dark skinned woman may be the one who gave the file to Ed or his partner."

"She might be able to tell us who employed her to do so." Lina muttered.

"I'll run that against our database of known vampires and their aliases."

"Thanks, Max," Lina smiled.

"Hey, Max, speaking of running things; the recently deceased prosecutor, Ramiro Santiago made a call this morning from his cell phone and it resolved to the name Chen. Can you trace it?"

"Chen? That's like the most common name in all of East Asia. Do you have a time?"

"Eight twenty one, this morning."

"If the moon is in alignment with the stars, I'll get something. Other than that, I don't know, there's a lot of ifs. If the phone wasn't a burn phone, and if Chen was spelled correctly or resolves to an individual phone that's also not a burn phone. I'll let you know on that one."

Chapter Eight

The court session took all day with minor breaks for recess. The waiting was painful and the lack of productive activities to perform left Alex with little to do. He passed his time tapping into the minds of those in his vicinity just listening. Once in a while, one of the felons locked in the same holding cage would challenge him, or pick on a lessor character; Alex was quick to put him in his place.

With court now over, he was being moved to The Wing, pending extradition. But it would never get to that. He was sure whoever was behind it all would try to destroy him well before then. He was alone and vulnerable.

He felt the onset of night. The wave of power waiting to

wash over him the same way it had done night after night for over two thousand years; a reminder that he was a true child of darkness.

The manacles were tight around his wrists and ankles. Chains ran around his waist to his hands, and his ankles were chained to each other. One chain was chained to the man in front of him and so on and so forth until the group of twenty looked like a slow moving caterpillar. The officers were not pleased with their pace. Alex wondered how many of them were first-timers like him, they had to learn to walk in a limited fashion. A free man caged against his will could go crazy in jail where ordinary rights have been removed. Alex shuffled forward, fighting the urge to break free and take Lina up on her offer to blow up all of South Florida, let alone just the cages that held him.

The first man was chained to the back of the bus and the last man chained to the front. The bus lurched forward, finding first then second gear with jerking movements. Armed officers stood at the front with fingers at the ready with loaded M4A1s.

The air thickened and the hairs on Alex's forearm rose. He gripped the seat, twisting as far as the chains would allow him to see the back door being torn open. Maniacal laughter filled the air. The bus careened on two wheels for an exhilarating moment before landing square on its side. Shards of glass flew everywhere. The crosshatched metal bars did not provide much shielding from the fast moving asphalt.

Alex heard the sound of bones breaking, as the men were bounced around like salt in a shaker. They were confined to their seats by their restraints, unable to protect themselves. A shard of glass buried itself into his cheek. The metallic tinny scent of fresh blood filled the air mixed with his bitter black blood. His canines responded as if on autopilot. Gunfire ricocheted around the tin can bus; an armed officer braced his leg against the roof of the bus and the top of a seat. He aimed at the being entering through the rear of the bus.

Alex gritted his teeth. Vampires. He inhaled their scent, rogue vampires to be sure. Rogue vampires were worse than dirty mercenaries. They had no care regarding the death count on their mission. They had one purpose - executing their target and they didn't care who, or, what got caught up along the way.

The machine gun fired, sending a stream of hot lead through the roof. Talons ripped through the officer's flesh gripping onto the failing shell of the man. Fangs drew the remaining fighting life from him. Alex watched the horror of recognition flood into the man's face. He was going to die.

The chain yanked Alex backwards, ripping off the seats. Gritting his teeth and dropping his fangs for a fight, he applied reverse pressure on the chain holding his anklets. He was able to snap it at its weakest point before the chain tied to his waist jerked him out the back door. He hit the asphalt and rolled past several lifeless bodies. Catapulting himself to his feet,

Alex stood on the asphalt listening to the sounds of the night. Three vampires remained and skulked forward with intent. At the same time, the skies opened up unleashing torrential rain matting his hair against his face. Sirens blared in the distance and bodies moaned beleaguered with pain.

"Who sent you?"

Chuckles sounded from the vampires as they closed in.

Alex scanned his environment; all the buildings had signs in Spanish. A traffic light pole lay crumpled on top of the bus. A fire hydrant spewed an angry geyser of water to meet with the torrential downpour. Men lying in the street spluttered, as the water level rose from poor drainage. Those clinging onto life, who couldn't find the wherewithal to move, would be sure to drown.

"I will make you one offer, and you have moments to accept it or I will kill all three of you, Alex said. "Tell me who ordered the hit and I will triple your pay." He smiled seeing one of the vamps falter.

The vamp on the left rushed at him. With his hands still pinned together, Alex drove them into his chest latching onto the black beating heart. Using the momentum, he swung one vamp into the other; the heart still in his hand. He sunk his fangs into it, drawing the sordid blood from its last few beats. *Either there is not enough blood to give me what I need, or this vamp was too low on the totem pole to know anything.* Alex switched gears to find the other two remaining vampires.

He saw the mortified expression on the indecisive vamp's face as he walked towards him with the cold calculated look of a predator. He was quite aware that the other vamp leapt up onto the wall to use it as a springboard. The vamp was now flying towards him. Alex jumped straight up, stretching his hands upwards, to form a loop with his handcuffs that the flying vamp's head went through. He sunk his fangs into his neck, while he used his chained hands to apply pressure under his chin. Alex searched for the memories he wanted while they wrestled mid-air. He gleaned that it was an internet setup by a mysterious buyer by the name of Chen. He severed the rogue vamp's head with a vicious tug on the handcuffs. Landing on his feet, he spat matter from his mouth and threw the dead vamp to the side. Alex spun around to face the last rogue vampire standing. He appeared quite nervous. Loud sirens sounded in his ear.

"I don't have time to run after you, c'mere, bitch!" Alex grinned, feeling unusually crass. He held out his hand in an invitation he knew the lesser vamp would not be able to refuse. To his satisfaction, he was propelled unwillingly into his grasp. Alex breathed along his neck, holding his head in the palm of his hand, he told him, "I haven't had a decent meal in days. I expect you would understand, right?"

The scared vamp nodded.

"You know I got what I needed and I don't really have a purpose for you." Alexander licked his neck before burying his fangs deep into the arteries. Drawing his blood and discarding the body moments before it ashed.

Alex fell to the asphalt with moments to spare before police cars pulled up. He imaged Lex and lay face down in the water. Blood streamed from his temple muddying the rising water. Alex made sure his image matched the other men that were still alive.

He listened as the police ran their checks; two of the inmates were alive. At last he felt two fingers pressed deep into his neck. The fingers seemed to be searching for something. He sent the feeling of a heartbeat and spluttered for effect. The fingers seemed to be satisfied as the pressure eased off his neck and the radio squelched before the officer spoke. "I got another one over here."

Max?

Yeah, Dad

The bus transporting me from the court to Dade County got ambushed.

By who?

Rogue vampires. An order initiated by a vampire named Chen.

That name again.

Again?

Miguel said that name came up on the cell phone as the last call the dead Florida prosecutor made.

Find him, Max.

I will, Dad.

Oh, and one more thing

What's that?

There's a camera on the building across the street. Make sure it didn't capture anything.

Which building?

I can't read the sign right now. I'm supposed to be weak and battered. I've just been put on a stretcher facing the opposite direction, but I recall a logo looking like a book with fingers walking across it.

A book? Okay, I'll find it.

Alex severed his mental connection and allowed his head to sink into the meager foam padding on the ambulance gurney. The feeling was borderline luxurious; it reminded him of just how accustomed he had become to the richer lifestyle. Even when he had been on a campaign, to rule the conquerable world, when it came time to relax, he always managed to find the luxuries afforded a king.

He sent a mental blast to the paramedic attending to him; he suggested that he was winded, in shock, with a couple of bumps and bruises, but otherwise, okay. The paramedic responded by giving him oxygen until he suggested some blood might be in order as his injuries were a little more than originally diagnosed.

Alex's veins pulled the blood out of the bag as his unnatural thirst demanded sustenance. Feeling rejuvenated, he lay on the gurney using the restraints to brace against the severe lurching of the vehicle, as the wheels of the ambulance consumed the ground. The blaring of the siren sounded like a sick melody; Alex contemplated the future that lay ahead of him.

Chapter Nine

Alex shuffled down the hallway in the form of Lex Macedo. His time in the infirmary had been short for a number of reasons. He could feel the night waning. The sun depleted his energy and the infirmary had too many windows to count. Staying there would require him to consume larger volumes of blood to maintain his charade. Being poked and prodded every two hours also inspired him to suggest to the doctor that he was well enough to join the general population.

He felt the guard's arm restraining him. Looking up, he realized they had reached a series of mechanical doors. The air swirled around his bare ankles and neck, as the vacuum between the doors released and the first door slid open. The radio squelched. The guard muttered a code into the walkie-talkie adhered to his shoulder then nudged Alex through the doors. Alex dropped his head to look behind him, the guard was following. The door closed behind them. The suction that made his ears pop, changed. The second door opened and a blast of cold air hit him.

They stopped in a short hallway that opened up to a large room. He looked around in amazement. The room was another holding pen. Beds were lined in rows. Men lay sleeping on and under beds, on the concrete floor and huddled up against each other in corners. The room could have been an ant farm for the amount of people being monitored remotely.

The guard released his shackles. He rubbed his wrists and rolled his eyes up to the large windows that would allow the sun to blaze over the room in a few short hours. Calculating the path of the sun and the angle of the rays, Alex settled on four beds that lined the wall that would remain in the shadows throughout the day. A tap on the shoulder reminded him of the officer's presence.

"This is how it works, Macedo."

Alex turned receiving the blanket and thin plastic mat pushed into his hands. He stared at the filthy items in disgust.

"Roll call is at oh-eight-hundred. Everyone here must stand and respond to their name. Once we have validated that everyone is here, breakfast will be served and not a second before."

Alex turned back to review the room.

"Got it?"

"Got it."

"Oh, and Macedo?"

"Yes."

"Don't expect a continental breakfast; this ain't the fucking Ritz Carlton."

Alex listened to the officer's laugh until the mechanical door sealed off the raucous sound. Another blast of air told him he was finally in lockup. He cocked his head, drawing a deep breath to analyze the various scents—a vampire.

He trailed the scent to the first bed in the back right hand corner of the room, under the first window. Strolling with a casual air, he stopped two beds from the vamp and used vampiric tongue. "Get up." Alex cocked his head in curiosity at the lack of response and spoke. "Get up. I know you aren't sleeping because this is still your time."

The vamp sat up. "Who the fuck do you think you are, telling me to get up? You just got here. You better go take that mat and go somewhere else"

Alex smiled, "I know who I am. It's you who should be worried. Your blood line is so weak I could ash you with a mere thought. You are so weak that you don't even have the skills to know when you are in the presence of a Master. You have no knowledge of our tongue. You are prey to me just like these humans that are littered about this room."

The noise of a mechanical arm moving caught Alex's attention. He didn't have to look up to know that the guards had pivoted the camera to watch the exchange.

The vamp twitched. He swung his legs over the side of the cot, "What do you want? I can't be in the light, I'll ash and I don't wanna die."

"You are young," Alex smiled acknowledging the change in the vamp's demeanor, "I don't want you to ash either, sleep under someone's cot. The fourth bunk down; the gentleman is already moving for you. I would hate to mess up roll call on my first day here."

Alex sat down on the cot. He motioned to the scared kid he had suggested to move, to come and take the bedding. He didn't need the warmth. While the temperature was a few degrees too cold for humans, it was still a tad warm for his liking; he still preferred his icebox.

Three more hours until roll call. He settled into the cot and tapped into the drifting thoughts of the men as they lay sleeping.

****

"I think I got it!" Max yelled.

"Put it on the big screen," Lina yelled back while pacing in the living room. She had changed into a comfortable pair of jeans and a tee-shirt.

The footage from the warehouse ran showing Alex fighting off the mercenaries.

"Freeze it!" Lina called.

"What's up?"

"About two frames back, I saw a face. Can you run it?" Lina peered up at the ceiling to floor windows that now displayed the frame by frame action footage of Alex defeating the vampire mercenaries.

"Oh, he's good," Max extended his fangs and chomped down on a bag of blood, "Go Dad!" he muttered with the bag still clamped between his lips, "I have all three faces running through our database and I've erased the video footage."

"But, Max, if you erase the footage somebody will be suspect," Jack called from the living room.

Max rolled back in his computer chair to look at Jack who was sitting on the sofa next to Miguel. Across from them sat Leonidas; Max cast a lingering glance at him. He was still uncertain about where his loyalty lay. "No worries Jack, I replaced the footage with one from a couple of days back and even dubbed the date and ran a batch program to work the time. It blended nicely into the regular morning activity. It's a pretty dead area at that hour."

"Oh, good job." Jack grinned.

Max walked out of his office, he tucked his keyboard under his arm for good measure, just in case something pulled up.

"So I tracked down this vampire from the drawing that Miguel snapped. She's from Trinidad."

"She's a soucouyant," Miguel interjected.

"What does that mean?" Jack swiveled to look at Miguel.

"She's a vampire," Max laughed, "I think she passes the test to be a vampire, which is pretty straightforward. If she requires blood for sustenance, she's a vampire."

"There are differences."

Max watched a scowl cross Miguel's face.

"Sure, there are differences; perhaps more like the variations you see in species than a whole different entity." Max grinned, hoping to offset the angry angel's glare.

"I don't think this is the time to quibble over whether or not she's a vampire," Lina interrupted, "we need information. I don't give a shit if she's the fairy godmother. I want to know what she knows."

"Right," Max stammered. He lowered his eyes feeling a little ashamed for goading Miguel into the mindless banter. "I think I've located her in Trinidad. There's one problem."

"What's that?" Lina asked.

"I think she may have a twin, because I'm finding a double across the world in Portugal." Max sighed, glancing up at the windows to check on the query he was running. Satisfied that the faces were still speeding by at speeds beyond human recognition, he turned back to Lina.

"So how will we know?" Jack asked.

"I'm thinking that we should go down to the police station and ask Louis," Max shrugged his shoulders gauging their responses.

"I agree," Lina smiled, "I'll head over there right now."

"Well, I was thinking that Jack and I would go over there and talk to Louis. You would attract too much attention." Max laughed.

"Me? Attract attention?" Lina smiled. "I know how to be incognito, you know."

"Yeah, well number one, you are Alex's wife and number two, you don't have a good track record at police stations." Max tapped his head watching Lina place a contemplative finger on her lip.

"Okay, son, you may be right," Lina mused, "I won't sit here idle though while you guys are out. What do you suppose I do?"

"You and Leonidas should go to the Vampire Council like Dad suggested."

"My data?" Leonidas asked.

"I did check on it, and the transmission appeared to go undetected. I've moved the data to an undisclosed location where I know that it's safe." Max stared at Leonidas. The ancient vampire's face was unreadable.

"Safe as in your Macedo network?"

Max felt a vein twitch in his forehead, his tongue twirled

around his retainer in annoyance. He squelched the rising burn within him. Leonidas was an ancient vampire; he could never win such a fight. He cleared his throat and forced a laugh, "Touche, I have long since plugged that leak and implemented protection from all approaches. The files are safe."

"I don't want Jack traipsing about the world unprotected." Miguel jumped up.

"Then you'd better be prepare to tag along," Jack laughed pulling on Miguel's suit jacket.

Max smiled. They had such an easy going relationship. He couldn't help but think of Sam and her gentle laugh. The way they used to wake up with her curly hair finding its way to his eyes and ears. He heard a chuckle escape.

"What's so funny?" Lina asked.

Max stared at her, poised with her one hand on her hip and face ready to snap. He waved his hand dismissively. "I was thinking about Sam, it's unrelated. Sorry."

"Oh, Amor, I'm sorry. How long has it been?" Lina smiled.

Max shrugged his shoulders. A quick glance in Leonidas' direction told him the old vamp had peaked an interest in his personal situation. "It's only been a month since we've been on hiatus, but it feels so much longer. I mean I've seen her since, but I miss just being around her for no good reason."

"When will she be coming by, next?" Jack asked, "I haven't seen her in ages either. While I wouldn't want to steal any time from you guys, it would be lovely to see her."

"Next week, and that would be great if you could be here, because we agreed that we wouldn't be alone for a while." Max sighed, ready for the attention to be focused elsewhere. "Okay, so it's settled. Jack, Miguel and I will go to the station first before leaving for the islands."

"I'm going to check on Archimedes then Leonidas and I will head to the Vampire Council." Lina raised her eyebrows at Leonidas.

"What about the data, do we not need to take them something?" Leonidas asked.

"I've prepared a folder based on the information from Miguel. " Max cocked his head feeling like the ancient vamp was definitely hiding something. "Lina has the file."

Max nodded at Lina before she disappeared. He smiled at Jack and watched her accept Miguel's hand. He could feel the warmth as she smiled and mouthed, "Give me thirty minutes and then we'll go." before stepping into his arms.

He nodded and turned to Leonidas.

"You don't like me do you?" Leonidas asked.

"I don't not like you," Max felt no urge to smile, "I don't trust you, but I leave your level of involvement to the wisdom of my step-mother and my father."

"You are quite smart for a fledgling and yet you accept her as your own?" Leonidas picked up the highball of blood he had placed on the end table.

Max watched as he swirled the dark liquid in the glass, feeling disgust settle in his stomach. "You are prejudiced against her."

"She is not a vampire."

"Yet, she has done more for this family than any other vampire."

"That does not mean she gets my trust."

"My father would not stand for any mistreatment of any member of his family."

"I would not dishonor my pledge to your sire, Alexander, but have a care fledgling. I do not take threats with an idle hand."

Max grit his teeth pulling on his resolve. He flicked off the retainer allowing it to drop into his glass of blood as he took a sip. The magic that suppressed his fangs, also suppressed the natural magic that vibrated within him. "I may be a fledgling in terms of the difference between our life span, nonetheless, I have only the best interests of my father at hand and I would die making sure that he and his honor were protected."

"And I am his oldest friend, would I not have his best interests at heart?"

The smile on Leonidas' face was unnerving. Max stood his ground. "You haven't had a heart for a couple of millennia now. With so much time elapsed, you may have forgotten the value placed on friendship."

Satisfied that he drew a growl from the old vamp, Max stood

straight, becoming confused when Leonidas started laughing. Not just a chuckle. Leonidas was gripping his sides in a hearty belly laugh.

"Now what?" Max asked, his frustration and annoyance evident.

"You are indeed you father's son. Alexander must be proud of you."

Max shrugged his shoulders, "What's your point."

"I can feel the magic rolling off you. You are a Warlock and yet a vampire nevertheless, with a will to protect those that you love to the death."

Max stood tall, "I would."

"Relax, son; I bear no ill will to any member of the Macedo family."

"Lina?" Max asked.

"I, like you, bear distrust for all those new to the circle of influence. But I believe in Alexander and so I will trust his wife, his warlock vampire son, the Peace Keeper and her Archangel. You all are a strange bunch."

Max laughed, "We may be a strange bunch, but we know who we are. Meanwhile, I'm still trying to figure you out."

CHAPTER TEN

Lina appeared in the hallway outside apartment she shared with Alex on the first floor of the Macedo Tower, in a section off limits to all employees. She reached for the handles of the double doors inhaling the scents that filtered through the cracks. The apartment breathed. She stood savoring the scents. A familiar, unwelcome scent filtered to her nostrils.

Anger boiled within her like a volcano ready to erupt. She changed her appearance into that of a school girl. She looked like an angry Latin Sailor Moon in short skirt, knee high socks and nautical attire. Flinging the doors open, she covered the distance with supernatural speed.

Her hands were filled with flaming red hair. Talons were

buried deep into the flesh threatening to break his skull. Lina's other hand stroked the old, decrepit skin in a sinister caress.

"What are you doing here?" she whispered into Ishtyn's ear.

"I'm here to warn Alex." Ishtyn hissed.

Lina relaxed the pressure on his neck, unwinding her other hand from his hair in a slow purposeful manner. She watched the old vampire stretch his neck and adjust his clothing. Her eyes were full of wariness though she monitored his motions. The slightest inflection or bead of sweat would betray his ulterior motives. "Do you not know how to use the phone?" Lina smiled after Ishtyn had finished his performance.

"My warning required a more sensitive approach."

A vein flickered at Ishtyn's temple. Lina licked her lips as the blue vein pulsated. She could take vampire blood just as easily as human blood. If anything, a vampire's blood held more allure to her. It was rich with stories and wealth that would surmount the often bitter and acrid taste. Old vampire blood was an acquired taste. Lina noticed that Ishtyn observed her attention. "I see," she went on, "so your warning required you to snoop around my husband's desk?"

Lina moved around Ishtyn like a predator surveying him from every angle until she was standing in front of him. She allowed him the full view of her Sailor Moon getup. She knew that he liked young vampires no more than fifty-years-old; just old enough to get a grip on their thirst and yet still young enough to have a hold on their humanity. A trait many vampires lost, overcome by the predatory instinct. She pressed against his chest until she felt him quiver, parted her lacquered lips and whispered, "I know your secrets, Ishtyn."

"No, you know nothing." Ishtyn hissed.

Lina stepped sideways. He maneuvered out of her grasp. She allowed him to face her. "Then explain!"

"I came to warn Alexander that Leonidas may be exposed."

"I wonder why it is that you bring old news," Lina closed the gap between them walking her fingers up his chest. She pressed her breasts against him displaying her well-endowed cleavage. A bead of sweat traveled down Ishtyn's forehead.

"Lex Macedo has been arrested," Lina spun around, "but you know that."

Ishtyn stiffened.

Lina smiled, reveling in his discomfort.

"Leonidas may have something to do with it. I only sought to give Alexander fair—"

"Leonidas? Or you? What type of disgusting betrayal would you have Leonidas embroiled in?"

"The Council knows of the leak and is taking measures."

"With Lex in jail, that means Alejandro is temporarily indisposed, and Leonidas' information hurts not only Alejandro but the Council; so what news would you personally bring to him and why? What's motivating you, Ishtyn of Cairne?"

He took a step backwards tumbling into Alex's desk chair.

Laughing, she climbed onto his lap; satisfied when he gasped. Her maniacal laughter filled the apartment. "I will find out what you know, old vampire." Lina's upper and lower canines extended, she chuckled, feeling Ishtyn's fear ripple over her. Fear was like an aphrodisiac. Each wave hit her like bursts of solar energy incensing her emotions.

"I'll tell you." Ishtyn stammered.

"Shhh," Lina placed a finger over her lips gyrating on his lap. "I know."

The smile that crossed her lips as Ishtyn moaned could not be called pleasant. In fact, it was quite similar to one worn by a serial killer just about to partake in some psychotic act. With her mouth full of sharp blood sucking teeth, Lina lunged at his neck.

The blood spurted like a natural spring into her mouth. Memories flooded her being. Images from the time that he was taken through to the time that he became a predatory killer. His innermost desires was revealed by each drop of blood that passed through her. Lina's eyelids fluttered. She read his blood searching for the one memory that would give her his truth.

Leaning back, she spat his blood on the floor in disgust, "You would betray your kind? Lest Alejandro?" Peeling Ishtyn's lip back to peer in his mouth, she confirmed the blood story.

"You are dying." She got up and walked to lean on the

peninsula of the desk.

"I am."

Lina watched Ishtyn sit up slowly, nursing the already healing wound in his neck. "Your body is cursed by a witch, which is why the vampire nanites cannot heal you."

"This is true."

"So you would give up your kind, your friends, for a chance that this person would give you."

"I... I..."

"I saw what took place with my own eyes, Ishtyn of Cairne. You best not lie now."

"It is true; Chen came and extracted my tooth with threats of taking the other. I can barely consume enough blood with the one tooth left. I need pure unfiltered and untainted blood to survive. I have grown attached to my life. There was a time when I would have traded this second life for true death, but not now."

"Yes, now you have land. Now you have a title. Now you have an appreciation for your immortality."

"Yes, and I am not ready to die." Ishtyn hissed.

Lina folded her hands and retracted her canines, having already wiped the remnants of blood from her face. "You do realize that everything that you have today is a result of Alejandro's kindness."

"I have made my own stamp. I do admit that I have received much from Alexander."

"Then you will serve a purpose still."

"What do you mean?"

"I could heal you. I could lift the witch's curse and even help you with your dental issue." Lina smiled.

"How could you? Do you have what Chen has?"

"Don't be an old fool, Ishtyn. Chen has nothing!" A burst of anger flared causing a wind to swirl around Lina and Ishtyn. "Do you think that anyone who wields that type of power would go around hiding their identity under garments? I know that you have never met this mysterious Chen, and yet you so readily give up information to an unknown figure standing before you."

"They had just pulled my tooth. I had no choice; they were going for the other." Ishtyn swallowed.

"I could give you strength."

"Name your price?"

"You will persuade the Council to support Alejandro. You will bind your allegiance to me. Every time the Council twitches, I want to know. And lastly, I want one of the heirs to your blood line to be bound in the same allegiance. The next in line, just in case something unforeseeable should happen to you."

"Done."

"Don't you want to take a minute to think about it?"

"I am firm in my decision. Please make it happen so I may make amends."

Lina rid herself of the school girl form and shook her hair

feeling free in her natural form. She pulled up the sleeve of her sweatshirt and glanced at Ishtyn.

"You seem rather dubious."

"Well, it does seem a little anticlimactic to be receiving such a cure and binding from a woman in a sweatshirt and jeans."

Lina extended a talon and ran her finger down the length of the underside of her forearm. She offered her arm to him. "Kneel and drink from the length of the line drawn. With each droplet that has formed, I want you to repeat your oath to me— I, Ishtyn of Cairne, bind myself and my heir in lineage to you, Catalina De Diablo. I pledge my undying allegiance to you."

Lina stared at the length of her arm, blowing on the wound to freeze the regeneration and removing any memories. Tiny droplets of blood welled at regular intervals along the length of her self-inflicted wound.

She watched as Ishtyn fell to his knees, drawn to the blood, "Take it and swear."

"This will cure me?"

"I am the Crowned Prince of Abaddon, my curse outweighs that of any witch."

Lina watched as the old vampire lapped up the dried blood, repeating his mantra of commitment. Before he consumed the last drop, she placed a restraining hand on his forehead. "Name the heir of your blood line."

Ishtyn's eyeballs widened, locked on the last droplet of

blood. Lina smiled, sensing his fear. He was so close to being made whole. This one piece of information stood between him and his survival.

"Her name—her name is Rebecca."

Lina felt his lips lock on the last droplet of blood. She laughed as the last few words of his mantra faded. The scratch she had self-inflicted disappeared. She grabbed Ishtyn's forearm and pressed her thumb into the underside of his wrist searing her brand into his skin. She walked around the ancient vampire staring at him as he rubbed his wrist. He elongated both canines and genuine surprise flooded his face. Lina decided to forgo her smile.

"Thank you," Ishtyn smiled, "I guess I should get back."

"Return." Lina stated, her voice quite monotone. She could see the surprise on his face when he found himself standing opposite her.

"How did I get here? I was leaving." Ishtyn stammered.

Lina chuckled, rubbing her hands together, "You see, you didn't just pledge your allegiance to me, you are bound to me in every way."

"Like a familiar, or one that serves?"

"Exactly." Lina smiled at Ishtyn's frown. "Everything has a price and you asked for immortality. You cannot pay the price with yourself if it is you who are on the receiving end of the bargain."

"I had immortality—"

"No, you didn't. What you had was an extension on life. That witch's curse was coming to a fold."

"What do you want me to do?"

"I want you to go to the Vampire Council and prepare for my arrival with Leonidas. I will need to address the Council."

"Is that all?"

"No," Lina smiled, "I want the Council to receive me, listen to what will be presented and after all is said and done, I want them to ready a solicitor to rid Alejandro of all these charges."

"You ask a lot," Ishtyn mumbled.

"As did you," Lina's smiled faded, "I met my end of the bargain. Look at you now. Your hair has luster, your milky white skin has youth - you do whatever it takes to meet my demands."

"I will see to it." Ishtyn dematerialized mid bow.

Lina turned to meet the opening of the apartment door. "Leonidas, what a surprise! C'mon in."

CHAPTER ELEVEN

The light streamed into the window giving hopes of warmth to most who lay shivering in the large holding room. Alex's eyes opened when the foghorn blared, piercing his consciousness. Sitting up, he swung his legs over the side of the cot and eyed the other men. They all stood in front of their cots or sleeping spots. Many stared at the ground trying to keep their hands and eyes to themselves. Alex rose to his feet.

He noted that a petite, brown skinned officer stood in the mouth of the hallway in front of the double doors. He listened to her call out names. She flicked through the list she had on her clipboard and checked off each as she went. Alex scanned the room, when like a stuck vinyl record, she got hung up on a name that didn't respond. Eventually, he heard a scuffle two rows ahead of him. He scowled when he saw inmates punched and kicked a man until he got up coughing.

Alex turned his attention back to the officer, who flipped her papers to the beginning and began again. He grit his teeth in understanding. The order kept in the holding pen was one of hierarchy, dominance, and control. The officer eventually got to the end of the list and breakfast was served. A metal cart with a squeaky wheel was brought out, and men went to retrieve a bologna and cheese along with water.

Alex took his sandwich and donated it immediately to what appeared to be a homeless man enjoying his stay in lockup. Returning to his cot, a change in the air made him turn around. His eyes settled upon two new inmates. These were cocky tattooed Asian men - Chinese. Alex sat down with his back against the walls staring at them. They made a beeline for him. He listened to the mechanical movements of the camera above him.

****

Jack looked around as she put her foot on the first step leading to the police station. Max was looking paler than usual, having applied a heavy layer of sunscreen laced with magic to help him against ultraviolet rays. Casting a glanced upwards at the overcast sky, she smiled, "You okay, Max?"

"Yeah, I'm good, thanks,"

He joined her as she headed up the staircase.

Looking around for Miguel, Jack whispered, "Are you here?"

"I am."

She smiled; she knew better than to keep looking for him when he was incognito. "Stay close."

"I will."

Taking a deep breath, she crested the top of the steps and walked through the arched front doors Max held open for her. Chivalry was not dead for the men who were not afraid to express themselves.

She threaded her arm through his, "c'mon, let's get through this."

"There are just so many people buzzing around."

She felt Max tremble. "Are you going to be able to do this?"

He flexed his jaw muscles and she felt him stiffen.

"Yes, let's do it."

"Okay, this way," she said steering him down the hallway weeding in and out of the milling people.

"Hey, Jacqui Brunson!"

Jack turned in the direction of the voice that demanded her attention, her eyes settling on Louis, Ed Trattoria's partner. A grin pasted on her face, she squeezed Max's arm to let him know she was letting him go. Waving, she smiled a smile the Cheshire cat would be jealous of, "Hey, Louis, just the man I was looking for."

She strode towards him with confidence.

"Jacqui, Jacqui, I told you, I'm the man for you." Louis laughed.

"So you keep telling me," Jack walked into Louis' embrace.

"I don't know why you stay after Trattoria."

Jack felt Louis give her a generous squeeze. She also felt Miguel's anger brewing. She released Louis, "Where is Eddy?"

Louis rolled his eyes, "Florida."

"Florida?" Jack furrowed her brows feigning ignorance. "He doesn't even like the sun. What is he doing there?"

"Ah, that I can't tell you," Louis chuckled, "police business an all."

"Right," Jack pointed her finger at him in understanding, "I was hoping he would help me with a case. Hmmm, I'm not sure what to do now he's not here."

Louis smiled, "Let's go to an interview room. Less noisy, ya know? Maybe I can help. Never know."

"Yeah," Jack smiled, "You never know."

Grabbing Max's arm, she set off after Louis to a nearby interview room. Louis walked straight into the sterile room leaving Max to hold the door for her. She smiled, knowing full well that reminding him that she could hold her would fall on deaf ears. He was raised by Alex and instilled with all of his old school values.

"Who is he?" Louis pointed at Max.

"I'm the son--"

"I'm not talking to you yet, son," Louis interjected.

"Look at me," Max demanded.

Jack looked at Max never having heard him use such an authoritative tone before. His eyes had blacked out vampire style. She turned to look at Louis, who appeared to be fixated on Max. She pulled the corners of her mouth down feeling a little impressed that Max had mastered such a technique.

"Please, have a seat," Max suggested.

Jack almost thanked Max for pulling out a chair for her, but she knew the offer was extended to Louis. The normally jovial detective took the seat.

"Jack is going to ask you some questions. Please respond to her with the absolute truth." Max said to Louis still using his vampiric persuasive tone.

Jack turned to face him and said, "Hey, Louis," she cleared her throat.

"Hi, Jacqui."

"Ed is down in Florida on the Macedo money laundering case, right?"

"Yes, ma'am, he is."

"What did he base his case off?"

"He's been researching the Macedo Enterprise for the past year, but he didn't get nothing until he got the Leonides file."

"Who gave him that file?"

"I did."

Jack pursed her lips. "Who gave you the file?"

"I dunno, this woman came up to the station when I went outside for a smoke and gave it to me."

"Do you remember what she said when she gave it to you?"

Jack watched as Louis moved his lips; no words came out. She turned to Max raising her eyebrows and shoulders in question.

"Louis, she can do you no harm. You are under my protection. Tell us what we need to know." Max sent Louis a feeling of calm.

Louis swallowed, "She asked me if I partnered with Ed Trattoria. I told her I did. She whispered in my ear."

Jack moved around to Louis' side and placed her mouth by his ear, "What did she say, Louis?"

Louis froze, "Hand this file to Ed Trattoria only, do not look at it, or speak to no one of it. If anyone asks about how you found the file, you will give them this description."

Jack listened as Louis gave her a verbal description of the hand drawn picture Miguel had taken.

"What are we going to do Max? We have no idea whether the description she gave him is her description or not."

"But we will."

Jack stared at the clear retainer sitting on the sterile stainless steel desk. Max's hand lingered by it. Shock jolted through her, "Max, what are you doing? This is too fresh for you."

"I can do this." He stared at Louis.

Jack thumped her palm on the stainless steel desk, "Miguel, help me out here."

Miguel materialized. "I agree with Max, the only way we are going to see what she actually looks like is if Max sees what Louis saw."

"Can you do this Max?" Jack tried to control her fear, lest that also made it difficult for him.

"Yes," he shook his head.

"Seriously?"

"I think so."

Jack threw up her hands, "You think so? This is a human life, you can't think so. You have to know so."

"Jack, relax. I'll help Max." Miguel nodded at Max.

"Have you ever done this before?"

"Which part? Feeding on a human or sifting through the memories?

"Either?"

"Sifting through memories, yes. I first fed on a horse and felt her memories travel in the blood; feeding on a human, no."

"Yay, for animal testing! Louis has less blood than a horse. Does that matter with the amount of time you have? Please be careful." Jack slumped in the chair feeling quite helpless.

Max nodded to Miguel and moved around to Louis' rear.

Louis seemed to be waiting for her next question. She

flinched when Max lunged, sinking his teeth into Louis neck. Her eyes followed a single bead of blood that created a path down the detective's neck.

Miguel placed a hand on Max's shoulder; Jack recoiled at seeing Max thrown against the wall with a mere flick of Miguel's hand. He sighed and placed his hand over Louis' neck to heal the wound.

Jack picked up the retainer and offered it to Miguel, who in turn offered it to Max.

"Snap out of it Max! We need you to take Louis out of the suggestive state." Miguel growled.

Jack managed a feeble smile as he wiped his mouth and took the retainer from Miguel.

"I'm sorry." Max mumbled.

"Is Louis okay? His expression looks so vacant I can't tell."

"As I figure, a vampire's persuasion or suggestion is almost like hypnosis." Max said. "He didn't feel a thing and won't remember anything."

Max moved to stand in front of Louis, staring deep into his unseeing eyes. "Louis, we are going to leave now. When you hear the sound of the door closing, you won't remember a thing except that you are hungry. Go and have a large steak for lunch, medium rare with plenty of carbohydrates on the side."

Miguel held the door open for Jack; she smiled, pushing Max through the door first.

"Oh, Louis?" Jack stuck her head around the door.

"Yeah," Louis looked up from the interview table somewhat confused.

"Just checking." Jack smiled.

"Checking?" Louis shook his head, "Sorry I feel confused, maybe I'm just hungry. Say you wanna get something to eat?"

"Thanks, but I gotta run. Rain check?" Jack grinned.

"You got it!" Louis leaned back in the chair.

CHAPTER TWELVE

"Can I help you?" Alex asked, lounging on the cot with one knee bent and his hands placed in a casual air resting on his stomach.

"Alexander?" one of the Chinese vampires asked.

"Lex Macedo, actually." Alex grinned at their confused faces.

"Alexander?"

"What do you want with Alexander?" Alex asked in Chinese.

"We have a message."

"From?"

"Chen."

"I don't know anyone by the name of Chen. Perhaps the message is of no significance." Alex smiled, waving one hand dismissively.

The shorter vampire grabbed the inmate out of the cot in front of Alex, while the taller one grabbed the inmate out of the cot across from him. Alex smiled even though their hands were around the men's throats and one quick move could end their frail, human lives. He already knew that the men held hostage were killers. He had no sympathy for them. Even so, he remained still, hanging his head a little to shield his face from the camera.

"You think that killing either of those men will make me pay any more attention? They mean nothing to me." Alex hissed.

The taller vamp twisted the neck of his serial killing hostage and the shorter vamp severed the head of his gang leader. They sent a mental blast into the room driving the inmates into a fighting frenzy. Guards came rushing in with shields and batons to quell the turmoil.

"What is the message?" Alex asked, moving to his feet.

"Chen says you should have more respect and honor for his family."

Alex chuckled, "I do not know this Chen. The message would have more meaning if he had hand delivered it himself."

"That will not be possible."

"Why is that?"

"Because you will be dead before the day's end." The shorter vamp flexed his neck cracking bones.

Alex chuckled.

"Why do you laugh," the taller vamp asked.

"Because you will be dead within the next five minutes." A sinister grin cracked Alex's face. He held his hand up palm facing toward the approaching vampires. Keeping his face tilted away from the camera, he lowered his voice speaking in vampiric tongue and began to draw blood from them until they trembled.

The vamps fell to their knees shaking one after the other. Their eyes wide in an almost unseeing stare, as their eyeballs shook in their sockets. The veins running through their systems dried up, causing the skin to wither and split. Their lips curled back revealing their teeth which began to fall out sounding like nails on concrete. Alex chuckled, recognizing the undeniable fear they were feeling as they accepted the end of their immortality. So many vampires and humans had expired at his hand; the expression was always the same, if not similar, when they finally accepted defeat. A look of resignation. The vampires exploded into ash and Alex found himself staring into the panicked eyes of the vamp he evicted when he first arrived.

"Enough," he waved his hand with an air of calm and the inmates instantly stopped fighting, falling exhausted where they had made their stand.

****

"So what did you see?" Jack asked. She stood with her

hands folded across her chest. His strange, quiet behavior was intriguing and yet annoying. "Max? Time is not on our side you know."

Max crossed his legs. He laid back on the sofa in his penthouse suite, "I saw the vampire. She is a soucouyant and hiding in the Amazon jungle."

"That's it?" Jack furrowed her brows.

"Isn't that what you wanted to hear?"

"Yes, I wanted to hear that you could find her and that you saw what she looked like, but now I'm trying to figure out why you're so quiet."

"I saw a lot of things from Louis' blood. Glimpses into his death filled life. It's just so morbid and I wonder if that's all in store for me. I mean, I don't want to be weak. I need to be able to survive and not be dependent on city life. I had a hard time in there. I think I could control myself, but I'll never really know because Miguel was there to save Louis. I won't know if I could have stopped myself."

"In time - you'll see." Jack stated.

"Time isn't my friend right now. I have all the time in the world if I can manage not to get killed. Sam's life is short in comparison." Max jumped off the couch and headed towards the kitchen. "The faster I can get a grip on this whole thirst control thing, the faster I can be with Sam."

"I get it," Jack cast a longing look at Miguel, wondering if he felt the same way. "Right now I need you to get a grip on things so we can leave for the Amazon."

"I don't know if I can trust myself out in the world," Max shook his head returning with a bottle of opened blood. Guzzling from it he sank deep into the sofa.

Feeling anger rising, Jack knitted her brows. She got up to stand in front of Max with her hands on her hips as she bent over towards the brooding vampire, "Didn't I just hear you say that you wanted to get this under your belt sooner rather than later?"

"Yes," Max sat up.

"Then get your sorry vampire ass up and put it in gear. Stop sulking like a five-year-old brat and help me save your father's empire!"

"Okay, okay," Max grinned finding his true nature from his depressive slump. He nodded. "I'll meet you in the garage in thirty minutes."

Jack nodded to Max before stepping into Miguel's waiting arms. She laid her head against his well-muscled chest and felt his strong arms envelope her in safety. She circled her arms around his back holding on tight. Feeling the familiar jerk, she knew that they were transporting somewhere. It wasn't like tapping a rift with Alex. There was no abrasive rushing of noise. With Miguel, it was remarkably quiet and peaceful to be in his arms.

She felt floor under her feet and relinquished the peaceful

feeling by stepping out of his arms. A quick look about told her she was in her flat at the Macedo Tower just a few floors down from Max's penthouse suite. The trip had been short, but the escape to tranquility in Miguel's arms had been gratifying. Jack smiled with hesitancy; she sensed that something was on his mind.

"Okay, what is it?" They landed near her bed, so she sat down on the edge.

"I didn't like the feeling that appeared when you met with that obtuse detective."

Jack stared at her stony-faced angel. "When I embraced him?"

"Yes, along with the exchange of words."

"That didn't mean anything?"

Jack leaned back on the bed feeling flattered, "You're jealous."

"I'm not jealous," Miguel puffed out his chest, "especially not of that rotund, balding man."

"Yes, you are." Jack chuckled, "Hmmm, what does he have that you don't?" she feigned contemplation as she placed a finger over her lips.

Jack's eyes widened when Miguel lunged forward with one hand on the wall and the other hand buried in the pillows.

"Woman, you exasperate me sometimes."

Jack gasped, his scent exhilarated her. He looked so earnest and hungry for her that her own desires responded to his closeness. "You know I don't want anyone else, just you."

He grunted, cupping her jean clad buttocks and positioning her underneath him.

"Babe, we only have thirty minutes." Before she could launch a series of complaints and remind him of her need to pack, Jack felt his mouth claiming hers. Soft, yet firm, with a sense of urgency that drew out the dormant hunger within her. His kisses broke down her resilience and within seconds she found her want met his own. Buttons popped as she ripped off his button down shirt. In moments, her t-shirt went over her head, his hands clamped down on the shirt restricting her movements. The need to complain was dampened by trails of kisses that rained down her neck making a path to her left breast. When Miguel peeled the demi-bra's cup back to reveal the pert, erect nipple. Jack arched her back, wanting the warmth of his mouth on her breast.

She moaned as the desire roaming the pit of her stomach spread like wildfire. Miguel made short work of removing her jeans. Jack's fingers fumbled with his belt as she kissed him. Grateful that he took over the removing of his own pants. She ran her hands over the length of his back marveling in the waves of his muscles.

She backed up further on the bed as the hungry angel stalked her. She felt his hand snake behind her back and loosen her bra, freeing her breasts. She no longer felt insecure about their size knowing that Miguel loved them as they were. All her thoughts were focused on the sheer pleasure she was experiencing. Wrapping her legs around him, she arched her back welcoming his fullness.

Breathless, she rocked her hips meeting his thrusts. The orgasmic climax came fast and they collapsed in a pile on the bed laughing; sated.

Her cell phone rang. She clambered over Miguel and reached over the edge of the bed feeling for the back pocket of her inside-out jeans where the device was. She squealed as Miguel playfully smacked her rump. She pulled the cell phone out of the crumpled clothes. "It's Max," Jack exclaimed. "Hello—yeah, we'll be right down—no, no we don't need more time, we're on our way."

Jack looked at Miguel, "Now that's not fair."

Miguel was tightening the belt on his camo pants which were tucked into socks and boots. He wore a revealing black shirt.

"Just one of the perks, my love." Miguel grinned.

Jack walked to her closet and pulled out her own pair of military cargo pants to be topped by a black shirt. She threaded a utility belt before outfitting it with her gun, clips, and ammunition.

"You are supposed to be a Peace Keeper, you look like a mercenary."

"Look at you Archangel you aren't quite the angelic image,"

Jack grinned and laced up her boots, "besides, I have all intentions of keeping the peace—and my life. I just want to be prepared. I'm not going into the jungle without covering my ass."

"Trust me," Miguel grinned, "I got that covered."

"I'll bet you do," Jack laughed. Running her fingers through her hair, she took some of the tangles out and gathered it into a ponytail. Walking into her bathroom, she grabbed a ponytail holder and wound it around her dirty blond hair. She looked at her reflection in the mirror. Her lips were coated in a pale blue metallic dust which also seemed to shimmer through the black t-shirt. Grabbing a compact, Jack dusted some powdered foundation over the angel dust. Once she had muted the color of her lips, she applied some pale pink matte lipstick, the typical color of her lips.

"Ready?" she called.

"Whenever you are."

She stepped into Miguel's arms and they teleported to the garage to meet Max.

Chapter Thirteen

"Macedo!"

Alex looked up from his cot where he had resumed his languishing. In front of him stood three officers, the one who spoke held handcuffs, while the other two positioned slightly behind him held their plastic shields. They reminded him of how his soldiers used to make a phalanx to penetrate the enemy's defenses; except these men knew nothing of the phalanx and time had not perfected the military art. "Yes, sir," Alex answered looking up.

"Come with us, the warden wants a word," the officer offered the handcuffs.

Sighing, as Lex would, he swung his legs over the side of the cot and rose to Lex's full height, which was just a hair above the officer. "Very well."

He offered his hands to the officer who immediately cuffed them and cinched them way too tight. He gave the officer a smile when one cuff bit into his skin drawing blood.

Without ceremony, he walked down the aisle of cots. When he got to the last cot before the rays of sunshine, the young, remaining vamp prostrated himself in front of Alex.

"Master, I'll help you take them down. Just tell me what to do. Just give me the word. I'll do anything that you ask."

"Stay in your cot, man." Alex raised an eyebrow. "What are you doing? Let me pass."

"Don't leave me here." The vamp pleaded.

Two more officers ran from the mouth of the exit and picked up the young vamp by each arm. Alex watched as he gnashed his teeth at them. He shook his head; the vampire was so young he barely knew what he was, let alone how to produce his fangs at will. He would never survive without training.

Alex bowed his head and drained the vamp of his blood. The mist of blood rose in the air hovering above his head. The young vamp shook in the arms of the officers. His bloodcurdling screams reverberated off of the walls of the cold prison. Alex sighed when he burst into ash as the light hit him when the officers dragged him through the rays of morning light. He looked at their confused faces. They stared at their hands then brushed ash off their uniforms. One bent to touch the pile of ash on the floor. Turning to the officer who had cuffed him, Alex said. "I don't know what you just did to that man, but I sure hope that you aren't going to do that to me. That looks painful."

He felt a prod in the back pushing him forward. No response to his question came, so he made a point of carefully stepping over the pile of ash.

The mechanical door sucked fresh air in as it opened on the other side of the lockup area. Alex inhaled, smiling as the scents of rain reached his nostrils. The simple pleasures of feeling rain touch his skin and wind kiss his face were burning his resolve to play this façade out.

Lina?

Amor.

I miss you.

I miss you too.

What are you doing?

I am being led to have a conversation with the warden.

Why?

I don't know, I'm guessing it has something to do with the visit from two Asian vampires.

Are you alright?

They were young and didn't have the skill to get close enough.

Who sent them?

Someone by the name of Chen.

I don't know that name.

Me either. It sounds vaguely familiar but not as they said it.

Well Max, Jack, and Miguel got a lead on a soucouyant contracted by this Chen vampire, so they are on their way to the Amazon, to track her down and check it out.

Max too?

Yes.

I'm worried about that. It may be too soon for him to be out and about.

He's a big boy, Alejandro.

Yes, he is my dear; he'll figure it out soon enough. I suppose Jack and Miguel will be there to help him if anything. How is our littlest cherub?

Darling, from our bloodlines, Archimedes is far from a cherub; but he was doing fine last I checked on him. I left him with Mirella and Jesus.

A nymph and a hell hound. What better babysitters could you ask for?

Speaking of strange visitors you'll never guess who I just caught red-handed, as they say.

Who?

I just...

The connection with Lina faded. Alex froze as he shuffled down the hallway. *Lina? Lina?*

Yes Amor, I'm here and okay. But I did get another visitor. Can I link you back?

Yes, I'm almost at the warden's office.

Another prod in the back brought Alex back to his reality.

He made a mental note to touch base with Lina again to find out about the strange visitor. With nothing to do for hours upon end, news seemed to be the key to focusing on the real world; one that he would cherish rejoining. For now, the warden would just have to keep him entertained.

The door to the warden's office was plain steel just like every other door in the prison. Unlike every other door, however, this one had no window. The officer knocked, cracking it a mite to hear the response.

"Come in."

Alex inhaled as the air in the hallway was exchanged and scents from the warden's office came rushing towards him. He smiled, delighting in the luxury that assailed his senses.

"Sit him over there."

Alex noted the warden did not look up.

He sat in the chair. The officers chained each hand and foot to the chair. He smiled again, thinking of how close freedom was to him at this point. Though the warden's office had the blinds drawn, two of the four walls of the office had windows that almost ran the length of the wall.

"Would you like a drink, Macedo?"

"Glen Fiddich single malt, 12-year reserve." Alex savored the air watching the warden's expression as he detailed the drink she had just chugged before he arrived.

"You have a good nose."

"I have a good many other things, too," Alex smiled.

"Are you flirting with me, Macedo? Do you know why I asked you here?"

"No, ma'am," Alex drawled, looking with earnest into the warden's deep brown eyes, forgiving her for switching the subject.

"Since you arrived at this facility some rather strange events have taken place."

"How so, ma'am?"

"Let's start from the beginning. The prosecutor committed suicide." The warden pushed on her index finger beginning her count.

"I've been thinking the same thing; that was unfortunate," Alex sighed, "did they rule it a suicide?"

"Don't play with me, Macedo!"

"I would never consider that." Alex stared deep into her eyes testing her resolve to see how easy it would be to persuade her should push come to shove.

"I noted how easy it was for you to assume the top of the pecking order in lockup without a fight."

"Do you find that strange?"

"I do."

"I have found that people naturally migrate towards leadership and submit to those more dominant. Perhaps that was the case."

"Then explain to me why two Chinese speaking inmates walked directly over to you as their first target."

"I have no other explanation for you other than perhaps they thought they exhibited more dominance than I?"

"You had some sort of conversation with them. I want to know what they said." The warden got up and walked around the front of her desk to lean on it.

"It was of little significance that I can recall." Alex flipped his hands with a casual air as far as the cuffs would allow him.

"Think, Macedo."

"They mentioned either giving me a message or making me a message. I'm not sure." Alex shook his head feigning ignorance.

"Is that so?" she crossed her legs leaning back on the desk to reach for her LCD panel. She turned it around to face Alex. "What the fuck is this about?"

Alex looked at the grainy screen. His head was bent and his palm outstretched. He watched as the camera panned to the Asian vampires shaking before exploding into ash.

"It looked like they exploded."

"You aren't fucking kidding me. That's three men today. I've been in the system for twenty-years, and I've never had men explode on my watch before. You come into my facility and I have three in one fucking day. How do I explain this, Macedo?"

"I'm not sure, ma'am, I would start with your officers. The third one happened in their hands."

"Are you suggesting that my men did this?"

"I certainly was nowhere near them, and your men are the only ones who touched all three of them, right?"

"You must be off your fucking rocker."

Alex sat back into the chair holding onto the wooden arms. He played with the intricate carving of a lion's mane at the butt of each armrest. "I'm not sure why you asked me here today. You seem like a woman of considerable intelligence, of which I'm in no position to insult. I would only request that you grant me a favor."

The warden laughed, "You aren't in any position to request favors, but I'll humor the request by listening. What do you want?"

Alex stared at her size eight feet in her black closed toed pumps. His eyes rolled up her lean, pale stocking legs - runner's legs. She must run several miles a day. Her dark green pencil skirt stopped at her knees, but not without hugging her form. Her white blouse was simple and parted only to display the camisole that covered her lack of cleavage. He parted his lips suggestively as he took in her form. Her natural red hair fell from its severe bun and tumbled down her shoulders.

He closed his eyes sending her a mental image of her in his arms. He watched as she appeared quite flustered and pinned her hair back up.

He sent her another mental suggestion to come to him.

Panting, she leaned over the chair. "I don't know what is going on here Macedo, but I warn you, don't fuck with me."

"What is your name, Warden?"

"Amelia O'Hara."

"Amelia, it could be a simple attraction."

"You are an inmate. I could never be attracted to you."

"That is an unfortunate turn of events."

"Let me guess, you are going to tell me that you are innocent."

"I may be guilty of many things, but not these charges. If you examine the chain of events, you might even come to that conclusion on your own."

"Not guilty is every inmate's song."

"I understand. Amelia, look at me." Alex lowered his voice into a persuasive tone.

The warden raised her head. He looked into her brown eyes. She was a lonely woman, her position of authority did not allow for too many relationships. Alex wondered how many men were intimidated by her. "Amelia, get rid of the footage of the three men disintegrating. It will not help your career. It will cast doubt on the facility. No one will believe you and your higher ups will launch a full scale investigation. These were murderers. Death in any form was fitting."

Alex watched how the impact of his words affected her. She seemed to be struggling. He smiled, acknowledging the fact that she was so strong-willed.

"Do it Amelia, destroy the footage. Send me back to holding and prep me for extradition." He smiled when she finally nodded.

"I'm going to have to send you to New York. If you are innocent you better hope the system works for you, or that you have a damned good lawyer who knows how to work it."

Alex nodded, allowing a half smile to lighten his face.

CHAPTER FOURTEEN

"Well, now, isn't this a surprise?" Lina walked down the steps from the office area into the living room to sit on the leather sofa. She smiled at Leonidas, as she pulled the sleeve of her sweatshirt down to her wrist. "Please have a seat." She motioned for him to sit on the opposing couch facing her.

Smiling as the old vampire complied, she crossed her legs. "I was not expecting you."

"I didn't think you were going to be here." Leonidas pursed his lips.

"You didn't think I would be in my own apartment? Yes, I suppose that is a strange concept." Lina raised her eyebrows.

"I just needed access to a computer station."

"It would be wise to be straight with me Leonidas. Max has an office with a multitude of computers. I'm sure he would have allowed you to use one if you just asked. I'm not sure that is a plausible reason. After so many millennia, is that all you could come up with?" Lina pouted.

"My future lies in the hands of a demon, a fledgling, an addlepated angel, and the Peace Keeper. I don't know any of you. I don't trust any of you."

"Yet you are here."

"At Alexander's bidding; I owe him."

"Now we are getting somewhere. I will forgive your insolence. You owe him?" Lina smiled.

"Yes, it's a long story that I'd prefer not to go into right now." Leonidas hung his head.

"What were you going to do down here?" Lina watched the ancient vampire narrowing her eyes.

"I wanted to see the child and look through his office for open ends."

Lina met Leonidas' stare, "My child? Be thankful that you did not. You would have met most certain death. In my absence, he is well protected."

Leonidas swallowed.

"You should get ready to head to Vampire Council. They are convening this evening."

"I am ready."

"Oh, and Leonidas."

"Yes, my lady."

"If it makes you feel better, we don't trust you either. I believe deception is an art, and you, my friend, are rusty. Even my fledgling vampire step-son doesn't trust you. Everyone can see you are hiding something. What that is, be sure I will find out." Lina smiled, acknowledging Leonidas' shiftiness. "Just know this. If I find out that you have betrayed my husband, or hurt my family in any way. I will kill you myself—a low, miserable death befitting every year of your existence."

"Do not threaten me."

Lina glared at the scowl on the iron faced vampire and gave him a wicked smile, "Don't think of it as a threat dear friend of my husband. Believe it to be a promise."

"Don't think I've not tangled with demons before."

Lina crossed her legs. She was used to being underestimated, "Leonidas, I know everything there is to know about your solitary life. And know this; every demon that you have encountered does not amount to a single bout with me. Trust me when I tell you that I am an experience that you do not want to have." Leaning forward, she patted him on the knee, "Now come on, enough chatting about your demise. Let's go talk to the Vampire Council and figure out where your dealings have fault." Leaving him with a gracious smile, she headed towards her bedroom, "I'll be right back. Let me go change. Sit tight."

****

The machete whacked at the palm trees breaking the low lying branches and cutting a path through the thick jungle.

"Wow, I'm still thinking about it," Max laughed, as he hacked through another branch. They had been in the jungle for a full thirty minutes heading in the direction of the soucouyant's lair.

"Thinking about what?" Jack asked.

"Traveling with Miguel is so different from traveling on a rift with Dad." He still hadn't figured out how to tap a rift. He could make a portal using magic, but Miguel refused to use them and in this case, they didn't want to get separated.

"I know, I was thinking about that earlier," Jack laughed ducking under a branch.

"Right, this is going to sound weird; being in his arms is so peaceful like. With Dad, there's this angry wind that almost blasts your face and I remember when I was human it hurt my ears."

"No, no, so not weird, you're on point." Jack laughed. "I thought it was just because I was biased about Mig. You're right; it's so peaceful being in his arms."

"Easy now, I'm right here," Miguel smiled.

"Wouldn't you rather us talk about you in front of your face?" Jack laughed.

"I suppose…"Miguel started.

"I think we're here." Max interjected.

"At the soucouyant's lair?" Jack stopped.

"No, we're at the base camp of the natives that are going to take us there." Max scanned the area below him where a few men were lighting torches.

"Why can't we go straight there?" Jack swat at a persistent mosquito.

"A soucouyant has several traits that are a little different from a vampire. It's those traits that will make her easy to find, hard to deal with, and difficult to manage." Max muttered, focusing on his footing as he slid down the small hill to the flat area where the camp was situated. Reaching the bottom, he turned to Jack and Miguel who were still coming down the hill, "We'll chat in a minute. Let me talk with the boss. Have a seat under those tents and I'll be back for you."

"Hey Joey," Max called to the figure in military camouflage pants and a black t-shirt.

"Max?"

"Yeah," Max grinned, extending his hand after putting his tablet under his left arm.

"Good to finally meet you in person."

"So what's the plan?"

"I'm tracking the sun as she falls. We have another few hours before the soucouyant will change. We estimate that she'll stop here first, because we are in the path between her and the nearest village. She'll need fresh blood to maintain her contract and we've got both human and animals here; quite the variety. While she's here, we'll be looking for her skin. Once we find it then we'll have our leverage. All we'll have to do is wait for her to return."

"When's that likely to happen?" Max rubbed his chin thoughtfully.

"She has to be back in her skin before the sun comes up. So worst case scenario, you'll have about six hours unless she figures out we have her skin. Then she'll return for us.

"Fair enough," Max rubbed his hands.

"Let's break bread before we go out."

"Sounds good." Max slapped Joey on the back as they headed towards Jack and Miguel. "Let me introduce you to my friends."

Joey shook Jack's hand and seemed to be all smiles until he turned to Miguel. Max watched Joey rub his hands on his sides. He raised both eyebrows at Joey in question.

"Max, is he an…" Joey started.

"An angel, yeah. Is it going to be a problem?"

"Yeah man, he is stinking up the rainforest with that vanilla scent of his. The soucouyant is not going to come here with him leaving that scent trail."

Max couldn't help but follow Joey's lead when he scratched his chin. He chuckled, realizing that he was mimicking him. "What do you propose?"

"The angel has to stay here. His trail leads here, so he should stay here."

"Then Jack should stay here, too." Miguel puffed out his chest.

"I'm not staying, I'm going with Max." Jack objected, "I'll be fine. When we have found her, we'll call you."

"Actually it doesn't quite work like that." Max laughed," Miguel will actually see her first if he stays. He'll be the one to let us know that she will be on her way back for her skin."

"Her skin?" Jack wrinkled her nose. "That sounds disgusting."

"Yeah man, she sheds her skin every night. By day a beautiful woman no man can resist and by night a demon that moves by fire and siphons blood to fulfill her contract to the devil below." Joey responded.

"A contract? It all sounds so formal." Jack looked up at Joey. "How did you know that Miguel was an angel? How come you smell the vanilla scent?"

Joey grinned.

"Let's just say that Joey is Sam's Caribbean peer and I don't think we should say too many more words on that." Max suggested.

"Oh, okay."

"Jack, you look puzzled. Sometimes in a land of magic, it's best not to discuss certain things openly." Max added.

"Got it. Oh, look. I think someone is bringing us food." Jack smiled, "I didn't even realize I was hungry until I got a waft of whatever they are cooking. What is that?"

"That is stew goat." Joey smiled.

"Goat?" Jack accepted her bowl.

"Yeah man, quite delicious." Joey grinned.

Miguel sat down next to Jack with a bowl of the stew. Max chuckled, "Can you even eat that, Mig? I have never seen you eat anything."

"Of course I can eat food," Miguel laughed.

Max shrugged his shoulders and accepted a coconut skin bowl, "Thank you," he nodded before turning back to Miguel. "Oh okay, well it's not like I can."

"True enough," Miguel put a well laden fork full in his mouth.

"Max what are you eating?" Jack asked, poking around in her bowl.

Max took a whiff of the contents and laughed, "Goat."

"Goat?"

Max chuckled at Jack's confusion, "yeah. Goat. Just not the same parts that you are eating."

"Whoa, I think something is floating in my stew? Maybe even looking at me?"

Max sipped the warm blood from his skin, relishing the needed sustenance. The warmth of the blood spread throughout him making him feel alive. It reminded him of how drinking an ice-cold beer on a hundred degree day felt; now the warmth felt just as refreshing. "Looking at you Jack?"

"Maybe you are the lucky one?" Joey grinned.

"Lucky?" Jack moaned.

"Yeah man, you get one of the eyeballs of the goat? Go ahead eat it. It's an excellent source of protein and good luck, I'm sure."

"Good luck?" Jack groaned, holding the eyeball up on a fork.

"Yeah man, you are going to bring the mission great fortune."

"By eating the eyeball?" Jack rotated the fork.

Max held his breath as laughter built up inside him. A glance at Miguel told him the normally stony-faced angel was having a difficult time keeping quiet as well. It wasn't until he glanced between Jack's miserable face and Joey's that he released his laugh was spraying blood all over the ground. Coughing, Max looked back at Jack, now quite cross. Joey and Miguel also seemed to be enjoying a good belly laugh.

"Okay guys, that's not funny." Jack was still holding her fork under scrutiny, "is this really an eyeball?"

"Yes, a little chewy, but nevertheless very tasty." Miguel plucked the eyeball from Jack's fork and popped it into his mouth allowing it to make a bursting sound as he bit down on it.

"Oh, that's just nasty. Make sure you wash your mouth out before you kiss me with that tongue. Gross." Jack pouted. "What about the luck?" she asked.

"That part we were just teasing about." Joey laughed. "Enjoy the rest of your stew. It really is good."

Max sipped the rest of the blood, watching Jack from the corner of his eye push her food around her bowl until she got the courage to taste it and eat the remainder with gusto.

"I think this will be a much better plan, now the angel is here."

Max took a step backwards, Joey spoke with his hands and his coconut skin of goat's blood looked as if it were danger. "In what way?"

"Excuse me, what are they doing?" Jack interjected pointing into the camp.

"Them? They are making rings of salt around the lean-tos and tents," Joey grinned, "they'll also spill rice at the tent openings, in any doorways, and on any window sills."

"Why would they do that?" Jack queried. "Isn't that a waste of food?"

"Well, the soucouyant can come and go as she pleases until she decides to enter a house with spilled rice, sand, or salt. We try to reuse the same grains every night, so we aren't being frivolous, but staying safe makes it well worth it."

"I didn't mean for it to sound bad. So, what happens when she encounters a home with spilled grains?"

"She has to count the grains. Hopefully she gets them all counted before the sun comes up because she needs to return to her skin, otherwise she'll die."

"Why doesn't she just stop counting?"

"She's compelled to count. She can't leave without counting. If she doesn't enter, she won't have to count." Joey turned, his island accent becoming thick, "Hi, hi, not this shack. Don't make no rings on this shack and don't pour no rice. No nothing."

"Miguel, I guess that's all you," Max grinned.

"I don't like the plan, but I'll go along with it. When the soucouyant gets here, I'll let you know. One question though."

"What's that?" Joey turned.

"If I smell so bad, what's going to make her come into the shack?" Miguel folded his arms.

"The inside of the shack will be painted in goat's blood. She might smell you, but she won't be able to resist the smell of fresh blood. The only thing we run the risk of is having her return too early, which may work in our favor if we already have her skin." Joey nodded. "I think we're all set then."

"Let's move out." Max rubbed his hands with anticipation.

CHAPTER FIFTEEN

J ack moved through the brush after Joey. He moved like a big cat, the epitome of stealth. His body weaved between the branches without touching them. She felt quite awkward trying to mimic his movements. The direction had been given—don't touch the plants. Leave as little of a scent trail as possible.

"What are we looking for exactly?" Jack whispered.

"Shhh," Max and Joey responded in unison.

Jack rolled her eyes, "I can't find skin if I don't know what it looks like," she mumbled.

"After she passes then we talk. Until then, silence." Joey whispered.

Jack nodded, listening to the screeching and clamoring of

the rainforest's night chorus was a little unnerving. Unlike the ordinary country noises of crickets and fireflies, these creatures of the night could be predators. They made the incessant sirens of New York City seem quite welcoming. The moon wasn't providing much light as the tall, towering trees filtered out any light. Even though her eyes had become accustomed to the extreme darkness, making out Joey's movements in front of her was quite difficult.

Seeing his hand rise in a still fist, which she recognized as a stop sign, she crouched. She made the same hand motion, so Max would know to stop moving. The sounds of moving brush behind her ceased. Staring at Joey, she saw him point at his eyes and then off into the brush. She ducked her head to gain a better view of what he was pointing to.

Jack pointed at her eyes and then at the beautiful woman who was walking towards the small body of water that lay fifty feet in front of them. The woman carried an empty platter on her head seeming to balance it with one hand. She had on a light cotton blouse which had seen many years; Jack wondered how it managed to provide any coverage as the stitching looked like it was barely hanging on. Her pale, creamy caramel mid-section was bare, skirted only by a length of material tied at her waist. As she bent down, the material parted, displaying a long, lean caramel leg. She placed the platter on the ground by the water's edge and began to remove her jewelry, placing them one by one on the platter. Reaching for the bottom of her threadbare cotton shirt, she raised it over her head. Folding it, she laid it gently on the platter. Her hands found the knot that held her wrap and unsecured it, pulling it until both ends were in the one hand so she could fold it and add it to the platter.

Jack dropped her eyes in embarrassment seeing the woman naked. She looked at Joey, whose eyes remained focused on the woman. He held a finger up at her. She furrowed her brows, not understanding what he meant. Shifting her weight, she looked at Max, who was also watching the woman.

She shook her head and hesitated before looking back at the woman who had now entered the pool. She was singing a lilting song as she bathed in the water. It streamed off her in rivulets as she walked out. Her features were dark, though not even the shadows could hide her high cheekbones and pillow lips. She had a slender frame filled with curves in the right places. Her ample breasts swung with each step. Her long dark hair clung to her. A breeze picked up rustling the trees.

Jack licked her fingers and held them upwards in habit, thankful to see that the breeze could not carry her scent towards the woman.

The trees parted, allowing a ray of moonlight to breach the forest cap. The silvery ray came down like a finger and touched the woman who let out a bloodcurdling scream.

Jack flinched.

She glanced at Joey and Max who were rooted to their positions, focusing on the woman. Ducking under the leaf again, she stared, her eyes widening to the size of saucers with each passing moment. The woman's skin split at her forehead. Talons extended from her fingers.

Jack watched in horror as the woman's clawed hands reached for her face peeling her skin like a mango. It sounded like tape ripping off a glass surface. As the woman doubled over, Jack knew she had to be in pain as the screaming commenced. She dropped to her knees placing her hands on the ground.

She covered her mouth to stifle a scream when the woman threw her head back. Her skeletal features were misshapen and not reminiscent of the beautiful woman who had just undressed before her. Bile threatened as the woman continued to shed her skin. She removed both arms, like a long-sleeved shirt and pulled the skin off her feet, which also had grown claws any dragon would be proud to sport.

Free of the skin, Jack watched the hunched figure reach for the skin. Her movements were awkward and disjointed. A loose tendon hung from the left arm trailing behind like a ribbon. She folded the skin with care; Jack shook her head in disbelief. She pushed her hand harder into her mouth just to be sure she didn't make a sound. She bit into her fingers forcing herself to control her breathing.

Fire exuded from her armpits leaving an after burn like a

flamethrower as she moved about. Jack watched her move a rock aside and place the skin with care underneath.

The smell of burning plant leaves filled the air. A trail of fire moved through the forest until it disappeared from sight.

"C'mon," Joey whispered, "we don't have much time."

"I thought you said we had a few hours." Max asked.

"Well, that might be true, but if something goes wrong we don't want to be out here without her skin in our hands. Trust me on that one." Joey nodded as he spoke.

Jack climbed over a large tree root and stared at them. "How could the two of you be so calm? Did you not see what I just saw?" she gripped her sides, "I still feel like I'm about to barf."

"Max, move that rock. It'll be too heavy for me." Joey said.

"Right, now I've got all these nano-muscles." Max laughed moving the rock.

"Oh, is that the skin? That's just gross." Jack winced.

"Yeah, missy, that's her skin." Joey grinned pulling his backpack off his back. Unzipping the bag, he pulled out some gloves and put them on. Reaching under the rock, he extracted the skin."

"It looks like a giant wrinkle," Jack swallowed, unable to turn her eyes away. She was fighting to keep down the goat stew.

Joey placed the skin in a clear plastic bag and sealed it.

"Is that like a big Ziploc bag?" Jack opened her eyes in in surprise.

"Yep."

"I don't feel so good."

"Take a seat there, missy; you'll be just fine now." Joey smiled.

"Hang in there Jack. It's almost over." Max smiled.

Jack?

Miguel?

Something's wrong, she's not coming to the hut. The old crone is hovering outside the shack, but she's not coming in.

Does it matter? We have her skin.

Excellent, I was worried about that. Well, I'll wait until she leaves and then I'll come.

Please, I don't feel well at all.

What's wrong?

I just witnessed a beautiful young woman peel herself out of her own skin. It was really gross. And if that wasn't enough, Joey just picked up the skin and put it in a Ziploc bag like leftovers. I'm just looking at my skin, like please don't go anywhere. Thank God Max doesn't have armpit fire; have to remove his skin, or any of those other issues. I guess I'm just thankful for what I know; I am just really grossed out right now.

I'm on my way. Tell them, she's heading back and just breathe.

"Hey guys," Jack called from her seat on the rock.

"What's up?" Max asked.

"I just heard from Miguel and he says that thing didn't go in the hut, and has turned back."

"Shit!" Joey delved into his backpack and pulled out two

more bags. "Jack get me a broad, flat leaf quickly. Max, fill this bag with water."

Jack returned with the leaf and laid it on the ground. Joey poured a pale sandy mixture onto the leaf. Then he took out another bag and poured a silvery substance on.

"What are those?" Curiosity got the best of Jack.

"The first mix is a blend of concrete and the second is salt."

"Why salt?" Jack asked.

"The salt will bind." Joey answered looking up, "Get behind me."

Max poured the water onto the concrete and the salt stirring the mixture using supernatural speed.

Joey stood with the bag of skin positioned about the concrete.

Jack could see the trail of fire moving towards them. The movement was erratic, as the fire zigged and then zagged. She flinched when the woman appeared in front of Joey. Hunched over, she rolled an eye ball over the bag holding her skin.

Jack sighed, feeling Miguel at her back. A wave of peace flowed over her. His mere touch steadied her and provided a ground.

"Do you recognize your skin, Crone?" Joey asked.

"What you want, Witch?" the woman lisped.

Jack was disgusted, she smelled foul. Her hair was matted and singed. Her once perfect teeth were now bloodied and filled with pieces of skin.

She closed her eyes trying to rid her mind of the sights before her; they just replayed like a thirty-five millimeter film whose reel got stuck.

"Give me," the woman hissed.

"We don't want to harm you. We just need some information," Max said holding an urn of salt.

"Death speaks," the woman hissed.

"I want to know about Chen," Max asked.

The woman shrieked, "Smash it. End it all."

Jack looked at Joey and Max. *Who could this Chen vampire be that the soucouyant was scared?* She stepped out of Miguel's protective hold and walked towards the soucouyant. "What did he do to you? What did he promise you?"

"Human blood," the woman hissed.

Joey opened the bag sending her wailing. "You'll not eat the Keeper, Crone."

"Wait!" Jack held her hand up. She watched the woman settle back into a pitiful crouch. "Did Chen promise you human blood?"

"Need human blood." She lisped.

"We will give you your skin and give you some human blood if you tell us where to find him." Jack told her.

"Skin."

Jack stared at her. Without familiar features, she looked forlorn. She looked at Joey who shrugged his shoulders.

Checking with Max, Jack thought she saw the barest of nods. "Joey, give her back her skin, please."

The woman took her skin out of the bag with a quickness and walked into the water. All eyes were still on her when she came out of the water.

"Gentlemen, avert your eyes, please," Jack begged, wanting some privacy for the woman.

"Not a chance," Max mumbled.

"It's okay," the woman answered with a thick island accent. "I'm used to men looking at me."

"Trust me when I tell you that I'm not staring at you because you're beautiful," Max mumbled.

"Then?"

The woman fluttered her eyelids, Jack wondered if she were trying to rid her lustrous lashes of the last droplets of water.

"I'm watching you like a hawk because you are dangerous."

Jack recognized Max's cold tone and smiled inside, knowing full well that the young vampire only had eyes for Sam. Sighing, she realized how much she missed her former assistant.

"What is your name?" Jack asked.

"Jezebele," the woman smiled, as she wound the material around her body and tied it at the nape of her neck.

"Where do I find Chen, Jezebele?" Jack smiled back. Her smile was infectious. She wondered if she should apply more caution and not look directly into her eyes. *Could she fall into a trap as she did when she looked into a fayerie's eyes?*

Jack watched Jezebele lower her eyes in thought. "I know he is from China." Jezabelle swallowed, "I don't know much that will help you, except that I overheard him say something about Xiamen. He was talking on the phone to someone saying he would return there by sun up. Chen is like this one over there," Jezebele pointed at Max, "except he is very old."

"Thank you, Jezebele," Jack said.

"You've seen Chen?" Miguel asked.

"Your scent is strange." Jezabelle sniffed the air.

"Have you seen Chen?" Miguel growled moving towards her.

"He stopped me in the market, I saw him." She nodded.

"Good."

Jack gasped at the sight of Jezebele's head being pushed backwards by Miguel's index and middle fingers. A bright white light shone at the point at which his fingers touched her head. She stared at his eyes, which seemed to be moving rapidly beneath his closed eyelids as if he were reading something or scanning something. His lips were curled in a state of disgust.

He released her by withdrawing his fingers. "I know who Chen is. I have seen him before. Alexander knows him by another name."

CHAPTER SIXTEEN

Lina ran her hands over the scales covering her hips on her demon skin red dress. The dress squealed in complaint when she squeezed into it. She positioned herself in the mirror to examine the little bit extra that stayed in the woman's lift of her otherwise flat abdomen. Did she imagine her hips were that much wider, or her bottom not quite as round? She bit her lower lip at the reflection.

"You are a sight of beauty my liege." Mirella laughed.

"You're too much, Mirella," Lina laughed, grabbing her bison pelt from the wood nymph to cover her shoulders; England is always so cold. "How is Archimedes?"

"He just ate and went down for a nap." Mirella smiled.

"Well, I'm off to the Vampire Council. I should be back before dawn." Lina smiled, pointing her toes into her Louboutin heels.

"Are you going with the old vampire out there?" Mirella pointed towards the living room.

"Leonidas? Yes, I'm taking him with me."

"You don't trust him, my liege?"

"I don't know, Mirella. I just don't know."

"So, why don't you bore a hole in his head and pour his memories out?"

Lina cracked a smile, "If push comes to shove, I might just do that, Mirella. I might just do that." She walked to the door as Jesus got up wagging his tail. "Stay Zeus, not this time. I'll be back and then we'll go for a walk." With her hand on the bedroom door, she gave one last longing gaze to the crib before pushing the door to take on her next challenge. "Okay, Leonidas, let's go."

Leonidas got up from the sofa not having moved an inch from the moment Lina had left him, "How shall we travel?"

"I'll take us there," Lina smiled, "it might hurt a bit."

Before Leonidas could object, Lina moved with preternatural quickness, latching her fangs into his neck while her dress squealed in delight as it absorbed his blood. While she gave Leonidas her version of a lie detector test, she teleported to London.

She appeared in an unused storage tunnel in the Underground system.

"What'd you do that for?" Leonidas rubbed his neck.

"I needed to know whose side you're on. I couldn't leave it to chance, and I didn't want to annihilate you on an assumption just because of a gut feeling, as they say."

"And now?" Leonidas doubled over touching his ankles where the dress had latched on.

"I see that the guilt that you are portraying is because you feel responsible for the interlude with the FATF agent that started the ball rolling on this investigation, rather than any involvement in the betrayal."

Lina watched Leonidas hang his head in shame. She laughed when he lunged at her, holding her by her throat, pinning her against the wall. Her laugh was high pitched. It reverberated off of the tunnel walls, sounding even more maniacal than it was. Her dress began to crawl up Leonidas' legs and her hands roved over his arms. "Silly vampire! Don't you know who and what I am? I could end you with a single thought, and you seek to try and restrain me? Not even my father can keep me in his clutches, let alone a vampire of your stature."

"I'm sorry; I thought I would bind you to secrecy. The Vampire Council would end my life for such a transgression. I have endangered all."

"Perhaps if you had maintained a better communication

with Alexander, none of us would be where we are. You should be old enough to understand that every decision creates a ripple that spreads like fire in a wheat field. Some subsequent decisions may douse the fires, while others may fan it into an uncontrollable monster." Lina smiled at Leonidas, "I'll forgive your momentary lapse, but you'll need to pull yourself together. What happens to you will be between you and Alexander. I try to stay out of my husband's affairs."

He nodded and moved a few feet back to lean against the opposing tunnel wall. He pulled on his linen jacket and fumbled with the belt holding his linen pants. Covering his massive chest was a silk t-shirt. It did his muscles justice. Lina smiled, Leonidas was an attractive man, in a big, hulking Spartan sort of way.

"C'mon, we'll need to get a move on." Lina trained her ear as the bells tolled on Big Ben. "Keep up."

Marching into the wave of travelers, Lina headed towards Westminster station. Leonidas shuffled behind her. He seemed winded. She walked onto a platform weaving her way along the crowd, skirting the walls until she came to the end where she paused. She glanced at the digital display and pursed her lips. The next train would arrive in one minute. The automated voice sounded over the loud speaker reminding waiting passengers to stay behind the yellow line.

"Timing is critical," Lina offered when Leonidas arrived at her side," Just as the train enters the platform we'll jump down, the people will be focused on getting on the train and shouldn't notice us jumping off the platform. We'll have less than two minutes to reach the door and gain entrance before the train departs."

"Right." Leonidas' inhaled a sharp breath.

The wind began sucking through the tunnel created by the speed of the oncoming train. Lina pushed the yellow painted gate and slipped through, as all heads made a unanimous turn towards the oncoming train. People jostled for positions on the platform estimating where the doors would be aligned. No one saw Lina and Leonidas slip off the platform swallowed by the darkness in the tunnel. Their supernatural speed got them to the door in no time.

"Leonidas, you seem winded." Lina smirked as she knocked on the door.

"Your dress has been quite thirsty, my lady." Leonidas stepped forward to respond to the doorman.

Lina looked down, "it is an undecidedly brilliant shade of crimson right now."

No answer came at the door.

"Step aside," Lina growled, feeling the wind pick up. She drew her hand back and launched a fire-ball into the door. It exploded off its hinges flying into the hidden hallway. Jumping up into the hallway after the door, Lina walked furiously down the corridor until she met up with four low-level vampires who came to investigate the intrusion.

Raising her hands, she compelled the first two to her and sunk her fangs into the first drawing his blood and then the second.

The two vamps behind back-peddled before turning and running.

"Excellent," she smiled, dropping the still expiring vampires and wiping her mouth in a lady-like fashion. She licked her fingers and walked with purpose; her dress squealed, complaining. It seemed reluctant to release the vampires as she walked over them. Giving it a tug to make sure it stayed with her, she moved up the hallway, realizing that they were heading back to the House of Commons, where the council had convened the first time.

She made it to the atrium. A young vampire pored over documents checking in the ancient heads of vampiric state, their consorts, and their representatives.

"Your seal?" the young vampire asked.

"I have many and am not in need of one today." Lina started forward.

The young vampire jumped out of his seat bowing, "My lady, the council is already in session. I'm afraid I cannot grant you access."

Lina curled her lip, "I am fed up with vampire formalities. I'm here, and I have something to say."

"But—" the young vamp started.

"Have a seat," Lina growled, pushing him with enough force that he went flying across the atrium.

She pulled open the double doors and gasps of shock rippled around the room.

Two vampire security guards rushed towards her. Raising her hands, each of them went flying backwards in opposing directions with such force that they became embedded in the wooden paneling.

"Sit down everyone," Lina strolled into the room swirling about to see how full of a council session it was.

Spying Ishtyn, she pointed at him. "Ishtyn of Cairne, I commissioned you to prepare the council for my arrival."

Ishtyn rose, "I made them aware. We were just discussing our rules on allowing consorts that are not vampires to speak."

"None of that matters right now. Leonidas tell them where we stand and then I will speak to you all on what I expect to happen," Lina snarled. "Should you choose to conform to your protocols, you may find your precious lives to be in jeopardy based on what Leonidas will now disclose."

Leonidas stood tall as he walked in. Lina surmised that he had taken advantage of the human hors d'œuvrés that were left back from the social hour preceding the council session. The color had returned to his face and his cheeks were no longer drawn and gaunt.

"Council Members," Leonidas began, "an investigation has been launched into various shell companies that were created to house the money we have accumulated in our extensive lives. The human organization, FATF and other human government agencies are scrutinizing every transaction."

The noise began as whispers echoed around the room; they grew into an uproar until Leonidas raised his hands.

"Please, frozen monies are only part of our problem. The information was given to the human agencies by a representative of a council member."

The noise level in the room flared again with the new information. Impatient, Lina stepped up on the platform where Leonidas had strolled. "Quiet," she yelled. "Look around at your peers. One, or some of you are not being honest and have betrayed your own kind. I say this not to create an unrest and turmoil, but to create awareness among you."

"Why do you bring us this information? You are not a vampire?" an anonymous voice yelled.

Lina whirled in the direction of the voice, "My husband is Alexander. He should be here tonight, but a member of this council saw fit to leak some information to the human organizations, and he has been imprisoned."

She spun around pointing her finger at the five master vampires representing the council, smiling at Augy, as the newest council member for Russia. "Two council members are not present. One I vouch for as does the human organizations. The other is suspect."

"What are you trying to imply?" the Sheik representing Asia asked.

He was a handsome man swaddled in his linens; his good looks didn't warm Lina's smile. "Imply? My dear Sheik, I'm not implying anything. I am telling you that the Chinese are involved in this leak. While none of you need lift a finger, I will find out just how involved. And when I do, I will remedy the situation as I see fit until Alexander has been released."

Lina watched the Sheik as he turned to examine the attendees. He nodded his head. "You do not live by our rules. How do we know you are working in our favor?"

"I am not, nor will I ever be working in your favor. I seek only, per my husband's wishes, to save his empire and stall his betrayal until he is able to return to the business of handling his affairs. Know this; he did not have to go through this for himself. He is preserving all of your ways of life by drawing out the enemy. And it has worked. So far the Chinese have sent two vampires in an attempt to expire him."

"What would you have us do?" The African Vampiress asked.

Lina turned to face the only ancient female in power, "I would have you send representation for my husband. Someone familiar with your affairs to release him in a manner that the humans would understand so they relinquish their pursuit of his demise."

"And what will you be doing?" The African Vampiress inquired.

The gold and black headdress perched atop the Vampiress' head was majestic, but it held no favor with Lina. She held all vampires that were too detached to make a difference in disdain. "I have, and will continue to restore the balance for Alexander."

The African Vampiress rose, "Then we need to take action for ourselves to protect our collective way of life. This task should not fall to Alexander alone or his lovely wife. We are each accountable and have a responsibility as leaders."

"I will dispatch a solicitor in the morning to Alexander's aid," the Sheik pulled out a touch screen cell phone and began tapping on the screen.

"Leonidas, you will work with my team," the samurai removed his headdress. "Perhaps it is time to decentralize our activities. Let us validate the integrity of our data and monies while constructing a plan that will withstand more contemporary scrutiny."

Lina felt a hand at her back; she looked upwards to find Leonidas towering over her.

"See, Demon Prince, we lowly vampires are not so bad."

"We will see Leonidas, we will see."

"I will admit that it is a shame that we could not reach this place of togetherness and union by ourselves."

"I believe that is an age old challenge across all species."

Lina smiled, thinking of her father. She felt no satisfaction having united the Vampire Council while the Underworld lay disconnected and dysfunctional. "Well, I will leave you to fixing the mess then, Leonidas."

"I suppose I ought to thank you for sparing my life." Leonidas whispered.

"Don't thank me yet, you have Alexander to deal with. I don't know how he will feel knowing that you allowed him to walk into that trap and then again allowed him to sit in jail instead of you," Lina turned to look at him. "You do realize that it is you that should have been in jail, right."

"Then I will bide my time until Alexander sees fit to pay me a visit."

"Excuse me," Lina nodded to Leonidas having been alerted by Augy that Ishtyn was slipping out.

She nodded her thanks to Augy and hurried down the platform walking out into the Atrium. "Ishtyn of Cairne, I think we should have a word."

CHAPTER SEVENTEEN

"Where are we going?" Alex asked, as he shuffled down the hallway.

"You have a visitor." The officer nudged him in the back.

Alex walked into a sterile room. It hosted concrete walls protected with many layers of paint, the last layer being grey. In the middle of the room sat a stainless steel table, which was bolted to the floor. Once seated, the officer removed one of the handcuffs and re-cuffed him to the table. Alex rolled his eyes; the whole experience was wearing thin.

He felt the weight of stares coming through the glass window across from him. He resisted the urge to look up and continued to stare at the swirls in the stainless steel, becoming lost in the patterns.

The squeaky hinge on the door to the hidden room reached his ears. He knew it would only be moments before he had company.

Sure enough, the door opened. To his surprise, in walked Ed Trattoria. He could tell by his unmistakable scent.

"Good morning, Mr. Macedo."

"Is it, Detective?" Alex mustered his best Lex Macedo voice. Every part of him wanted to be done with jail and all of the inconsistent processes associated with it. He watched the detective take a seat and open the file with grand ceremony, thumbing through the pages to bide time.

Having no control over the length of time they were to spend, he decided to offer responses when requested.

"I understand that this way of life is very different from what you must be accustomed." Ed Trattoria smiled.

"Are you toying with me, Detective? If so, I really can't sustain such conversations." Alex controlled his many urges just to walk out of there. The metal handcuffs were of no consequence. Making an exit through one of the windows was a non-issue as was the potential for jumping four floors down.

"Are you in a rush to get somewhere, Mr. Macedo?"

"I am not permitted to control my own clock in this facility. Was there a purpose for this meeting today Detective, or did you just want to check up on my agenda?" Alex snapped.

"I heard about the incidences today."

"News travels fast."

"We are going to get you to New York."

"I think I would prefer to get there under my own steam, thank you. The government's mode of transportation has proven to be quite unreliable."

"Under your own steam?" Ed raised an eyebrow.

"I don't plan on being in the system for much longer."

"Planning an escape then?"

"Not exactly," Alex smiled, "my escape will be the truth. I have committed no crime whether direct or indirect."

"We'll see about that, Mr. Macedo," Ed shook his head, "I have a file here."

"Mr. Trattoria, I think you have made a decision somewhere along the line to target my family for one reason or another. A jilted lover perhaps? Did I not hear that you had hoped for a relationship with Jacqui Brunson? Now that she is dating Miguel D'Angelo and residing in the Macedo Tower, maybe you feel a little cut off or rejected. And as for your file; did it occur to you that maybe someone has filled a folder with some cockamamie stories for you to latch onto to so that you can do their dirty work?"

"Pleading innocence, Mr. Macedo?"

"There'll be no pleading necessary. The truth will become apparent soon. What will happen to your career when your higher ups realize that you have dedicated tax payer's money targeting an unfounded lead of an established law-abiding citizen?"

"I do not have to explain my actions to you."

"But you do find yourself wondering, don't you, Mr. Trattoria? Is that why you are here today? What will you tell them? Should they launch an internal investigation regarding you actions in conjuction with those of the FATF? How will you confirm that you have done your due diligence?"

"You will be placed in isolation for your own protection until we are ready for transport."

"Why deliver that inconsequential message personally, Trattoria?" Alex questioned, "Do all of your inmates get such preferential treatment?"

"You are a little pricklier than I thought you'd be, Macedo."

"I won't apologize for not bending all the way over for you, Trattoria. I will say this though, when I get out of here and I will… I will exercise my rights to the full extent of the law."

"While that may be so, I have a couple of questions for you, if you don't mind. How long have you known Leonides Brown?" he asked, looking through the file.

Alex smiled, "I think our conversation has gone on for way too long. Not once since I was collected and detained has anyone offered a phone call."

"How did you get to Leonides Brown's house? We have no log of any vehicle arriving or departing."

"Perhaps yet another oversight on your organization's part; I'm sure there are many who could not explain the level of neglect or misdirection. I was also denied my right to a phone call." Alex smiled, staring at Ed intently. His greasy hair was slicked back. As he grew agitated, a vein pulsated in his temple. Alex watched it blinking slowly until he felt the tingle hit him from the draw. He realized that he had begun feeding on Ed. Shaking his head, he cleared his mind. Ed seemed to fall forward bracing his arms onto the steel table for support. "Everything alright, Detective?"

Ed Trattoria turned to look at the glass. He raised his left hand and closed the file. "Excuse me." He got up and knocked on the door for the guard to open it.

Alex heard Trattoria whisper one word to the guard, 'isolation' before shuffling off.

CHAPTER EIGHTEEN

"So we know the guy?" Max swatted at a mosquito.

"Yes, he is the offspring of Qin Shi Huang." Miguel folded his arms.

"So what does that mean?" Jack asked, using both hands to smack the mosquitoes that kept landing on her.

"That means we go to China and we go find this mysterious Chen." Miguel kicked at the dirt with his right foot.

"What's his real name?" Max asked.

"He was named after his father, Zheng."

"I thought you said his father was Qin Shi Huang?" Jack asked.

"Those are his royal names, his given name was Zheng."

Max stared at Miguel thinking that his pose was unusually defensive. "You're holding something back. What is it?"

Miguel unfolded his arms letting out a deep sigh, "The Chinese are a very old family."

"And?" Max sipped from a coconut skin while Miguel pondered. "C'mon Mig, just spit it out."

"So the objective is to find Chen and do what?"

"Find him and get him to stop targeting Dad! I'm surprised that you would even ask such a question. I'm confused." Max threw his hands up.

"I'm just saying it's not our fight."

"What's that mean, Mig, not our fight? I would fight for my father until the end." Max gritted his teeth.

"Well, you'll meet your end for sure sooner rather than later if you go to China." Miguel held his hand out, "I'm just suggesting that its time Alexander see this through. We know who is behind it all."

"So that's it?"

"I'm here to protect Jack. She shouldn't be involved in this until it is brought to her court. The only one with the strength to stand up to the Chinese vampires out of the three of us is me, Max. I'm not tooting my own horn, but you have to figure it out for a few more years before you can take on their lowest level vamp. Alexander wouldn't want you on a suicide mission. I'm sure that's not his intent."

"So what are you suggesting?"

"I'm suggesting we go back to the Macedo Tower and wait for Lina. Then we get Alex out of jail and allow him to manage his business.

"Okay, we'll run things per your suggestion," Max turned to Jack, "you've been awful quiet during his deliberation, cat got your tongue?"

"I think he may be right," Jack swallowed, "while I'd like to run off. I think this may be beyond our collective abilities."

"Wow! Okay," Max's eyes flit between Jack and Miguel, scanning them for signs of malice. "Why don't the two of you head back to the Tower, I'll follow shortly. I just want to tie up a couple of loose ends here and I'll be right along."

"How will you get back?" Jack asked, stepping into Miguel's arms.

"I can draw up a portal as well as the next," Max grinned.

He watched Miguel wrap his wings around Jack and disappear.

"You're not going to New York, are you?"

"Joey," Max spun around the grin faded, "how long were you there listening?"

"Long enough." Joey shook his head, "I know you well enough to believe that you are not going to head back."

"I'm going to the Tower; after I hit China. I have to give it a shot."

"There's some truth in what he says, you know?"

"I know, but I know my Dad would fight for me til he couldn't fight any more. I would do the same for him."

"Yeah man, but there are other ways to prove to him that you are truly his son."

"Joey, this is not about proving anything."

"I hope not Max, because he already knows you are his son. Something inside him would die if he lost you."

"I won't die Joey. Why does everyone underestimate me?" Max shook his head in disbelief. Some amount of frustration set in. As a human, he had been glued to the computer and underestimated in every forum, except those technology related.

"Is not no one underestimating you man, we just know what those Chinese vamps are about."

"I gotta try."

"Be safe, man."

Max shook Joey's hand before reaching into his pocket. He brought out a jar of pre-mixed herbs. A series of chuckles broke his concentration. Looking up, he saw Joey leaning against a tree watching him with intent.

"Still practicing, huh?" Joey laughed.

"Now more than ever, I feel the magic flowing stronger than before in my blood." Max sprinkled the herbs about him in a circle. He spun in slow motion chanting just under his breath.

Max closed his eyes listening to the wind rustling through the leaves. He felt the drain of sunrise. The day was almost upon him. His eyes flew open at the sound of a horn blaring. A deep searing pain brought awareness to him. Looking around, he realized the sun had not quite set in China. Stifling a scream, he scanned the area for shadows which were plenty and long. Using his supernatural speed, he ducked behind a building. Once in the safety of the shadows, Max leaned against the wall of the building to feel cool and ease the pain that had ignited over him. He crouched down, panting out of habit. Alex's voice permeated into his consciousness reminding him that breathing was no longer a requirement for anything other than speaking. He slowed his breathing and cleared his mind. Patting the legs of his pants, he pulled out his cell phone.

"Let me figure out where I am and do a search," He hit his head with an open palm waiting for the phone to load his home-grown application. "This was so impulsive; I could have done better with some planning. Dammit. Maybe I did run off a little half-baked. Damn!"

"What do we have here?"

Max turned his head in the direction of the voice. From his position, he saw five sets of expensive leather shoes. Not being a real aficionado for expensive footwear, Max could tell when they were out of his price range. He was finding out though, cheap clothes didn't last immortals a long time, which was why everyone always appeared so well dressed.

Soon the shoes got closer. Max could see that they were hand-made. Pale blue silk pants with a deep conventional break topped the shoes. A mandarin collared jacket of the same material and color topped the pants. Max continued to look up until he found the distasteful smile of a Chinese vampire looking down at him. An intricate antique walking stick was poised between him and the vamp.

"Hi," Max gave a slight awkward wave. He rose. Not being a tall man, he was always shocked to find other men of the same or shorter size.

"Oh, oh, an American," the Chinese vampire dipped. He emphasized the word American with a thick Chinese accent. He lengthened the word with what Max felt was a sincere deep-rooted disgust for all things American.

"Yes, my name is Maxwell Macedo. How are you? What's your name?" Max offered his hand in greeting and pasted an affable all-American smile on his face.

If pleasantries existed before, they were dropped. The Chinese vamp's face was as dispassionate as a stone statue, void of any expression. "What are you doing here, Macedo?"

"I came here with hopes to speak to Chen."

One of the vampires in the entourage chuckled. For the first time, Max gave them a look. They were all dressed in black. *Stooges*, he thought. *Armed goons who will definitely lay a hurting on me if I don't think of something fast.*

"Either your fortune or misfortune has worked in your favor

today, Macedo. I am the one they call Chen."

Max's eyes opened wide, he couldn't move fast enough to avoid Chen. He felt the strength of the vampire gripping him like a vice. Fangs pierced his neck, sending a burning sensation arcing throughout him. Pinpoints of electricity sizzled in his skull from Chen's talons.

He heard a scream; it seemed to start like a groan and then grew into a full-blown scream. His body was bent backwards; Max felt the world slipping away. He realized that the second scream was his own. His eyes rolled backwards, feeling the whisk of being teleported. He released his grip on his mobile phone and didn't hear it hit the ground.

CHAPTER NINETEEN

The Corinthian leather on the ladder back chair in the judge's chambers was well received by Lina. She smiled, crossed her legs and was thankful for her wardrobe choice. She had opted for an easy gunmetal blue ruched faux wrap dress that moved with her; the perfect complement for hot and sticky south Florida weather.

She eyed the lawyer the Sheik had assigned to Alexander's case. Vampire etiquette wasn't always so stifling; there were times that she found some of the traditions quite intriguing. Seeing the Sheik call upon his familiar was a treat. The lawyer was bound to the Sheik in every way. No fear dilated through his eyes when the Sheik told him what was required of him. Like an obedient dog with intelligence, he listened and obeyed.

Lina had chartered a jet to transport them both from the UK to south Florida. She had been pleased to see the lawyer researching information the entire flight. She had given him the privilege of seeing all that Miguel had photographed from the file. Watching him now, as he stood at Judge Sander's desk waiting for her to arrive, he flipped through his file, thumbing each page with a slow purpose. He was a man of small stature and quite odd to look at. His nose was long and narrow, coming to a point over a prominent chin. His brows were just as untamed as the hair on his head and for a man standing at the same height as her - sans her five inch heels, he had the air of confidence that the Napoleonic stereotype would require.

The prosecutor, on the other hand, seemed unnerved by his presence. Crossing her legs in the other direction so she could get a close look at the man, she realized that he could be nervous because he was young and fresh.

She watched him turn to look at her. Smiling, she parted her lacquered lips as if she were about to whisper something quite personal to him. She had pinned her hair up, but decided now that she had his attention she'd remove the pin. Its removal sent her hair tumbling down about her shoulders with a little shake of her head. Closing her eyes, she sent her hair into action and the dark, lustrous tresses fell.

When she opened her eyes, Lina knew that she had the young

prosecutor hooked. She felt the lawyer turn and wondered if he had been watching her. She dare not lose contact with the prosecutor. A bead of sweat appeared on his brow. His nervous hand reached up to wipe it away.

"Holy shit! What a day!" the Judge stormed into her chambers.

The prosecutor jumped up.

"Sit, sit, sit!" Judge Sanders waived her hand in dismissal of the formality.

"You'll never believe the day I've had," Judge Sanders blew her graying brown hair out of her face, moving a stubborn tress with her hand, tucking it behind her ear. Looking up, Lina watched her eyes roam from the prosecutor to the lawyer, passing over her before finally resting on the file in front of her. "So what are we talking about today?"

The prosecutor seemed to fumble with the file before turning it over to the Judge, "Judge this meeting was called regarding the Macedo file."

"Macedo? He's still in Florida; I thought that he was going to be extradited to New York City."

"If I may?" the lawyer poised a finger in the air.

"Who are you?" Judge Sanders turned to the lawyer.

"My name is Aloysius Waechter, I am legal counsel for Mr. Lex Macedo," the lawyer responded.

"What are you here to discuss?"

"My client's release?" Aloysius answered.

"I'm not sure that is within my jurisdiction."

"He is being held within your jurisdiction."

Lina watched Judge Sanders turn towards the prosecutor and threw her hands in the air.

"If I may also add, my client was detained by FATF on a warrant on which he was not named. He was read his rights some time later by a New York police officer working as a liaison to the FATF, quite after the fact; and then detained in Miami holding without due process. So far my client has received poor protection while he has been in custody. He has been subject to life threatening attacks in two instances and mental trauma. To add insult to injury, he has been denied bail and his right to counsel."

"What are you suggesting Counsel?"

"I'm suggesting that he be released on his own recognizance."

"We don't generally do that down here, Counsel. We usually have bail set."

"Under the circumstances you have nothing to set bail for, your Honor. Additionally, it is my understanding that this is an international investigation meaning that the trial won't be taking place in your court room."

Lina cocked her head seeing that a strange contemplative look crossed the Judge's face.

"So, you will guarantee that Mr. Lex Macedo will appear in

court wherever it will be held?" Judge Sanders queried, pointing at Aloysius Waechter.

"I assure you that should a trial come to fruition, Mr. Lex Macedo will be present."

"Prosecutor Gaines, you have been quiet on the matter."

"Judge, the State of Florida has nothing because it was not our investigation. We merely provided a function for the FATF. Should they not have crossed their t's and dotted their i's, it is our position that Mr. Macedo be released period. If the FATF has something that they would like to try Mr. Macedo for, we recommend that they produce subsequent documentation requiring Mr. Macedo's appearance for trial in the state, county, or country of their choosing for whatever charges that they finally derive."

Lina stifled a chuckle seeing the prosecutor release a deep sigh at the close of his deliberation. The Judge rifled through the paperwork one last time before closing the file then said, "Okay, I'll release him. Just make sure he shows up and never comes back here."

CHAPTER TWENTY

The rat sniffed the ground avoiding the large puddle that pooled around the base of the toilet. Alex watched it look upwards at the natural light filtering into the small cell. He lay on the cot for hours in the same position with his hands behind his head. Once in a while, a tray would grate against the ground as it slid through the door. A metal plate would slide backwards as an officer peered in at him. At first he looked back at the officer. Thereafter, he didn't bother to get up and refused any item on the tray.

The isolation cell was filled with scents of blood, feces, and stale urine. The walls hosted a series of scratches. Alex presumed them to be a tabulation of days. He remembered rubbing his finger in the crevices of the scratches. The scents left on his fingers were that of stale blood. So many stories were left untold in the room.

He swung his legs over the side of the cot at the sound of the mechanical lock sliding. A suction of fresh air burst into the decay filled room.

"Macedo?"

"I'm still the only one that you locked in this room."

"Get up." The officer demanded.

"Where to now?"

"Apparently you are going home." The officer snarled.

"Finally," Alex grinned and stood up.

"Hands." The officer held up a pair of handcuffs.

"But I'm being released." Alex objected.

"You are as trustworthy as the next convict until you reach the front gate where you can walk out under your own steam. "

Alex growled, annoyed, yet presenting his hands, "Let's make this as quick and painless as possible."

He shuffled down a never-ending hallway followed by his armed entourage. They made several turns before ending up at an elevator which dumped him out on the second floor. He paused at a pass through where he would be processed before leaving the facility. While he was waiting for the cuffs and chains to be removed, an officer walked up to him and whispered.

"Macedo?"

"Yes."

"I have a message for you."

"Speak." Alex lowered his voice.

"I have your son."

Alex turned his head to look at the officer. "What?"

The officer looked at Alex and pushed him backwards, "What are you doing inmate?"

He chose not to respond. Looking at the officer, he realized that the man would have no inkling or recollection of the message he just conveyed. He was used as a pawn.

"Joe, stop pushing Macedo around and bring me those cuffs." Another officer called.

"He just stepped in my face."

"Actually, Joe, you walked up to him."

"No, I didn't."

"Gentlemen, my cuffs please." Alex asked, presenting his hands.

Joe reluctantly moved forward. Alex wanted the possession to occur again so he could ask which son, and who sent the message. Few people knew of Archimedes; he assumed it was Max.

Does it matter which son? My actions would be the same for either. But if it were Max, he is a grown adult—and a fledgling vampire which equates to a small child against an ancient. He does have the some magic— then again, he has no real experience as a vampire—either way it's an awful situation. Alex gritted his teeth. *I will kill whoever is responsible for messing with my family.*

He stripped out of his orange jumpsuit still preoccupied with the need to protect his family, signed for his belongings in silence and checked the time before he started out of the facility. The sun was just setting.

He turned on his cell phone and reached out for Lina mentally:

Lina?

Amor?

Where are you?

In the limo outside.

Which entrance?

The front.

Alex walked outside, shielding his eyes from the last rays of light stretching across the sky. He hurried down the front steps and into the waiting limo.

"Amor," Lina smiled.

Alex crushed her words with a passionate kiss, relinquishing the façade of Lex. His hands wove their way through the thick tresses of her illustrious wavy hair. Her scent was so rich of death; heightened no doubt by excitement. He could barely contain his wants. His fangs dropped.

The sound of someone clearing their throat threw Alex back to his own side of the limo. Staring at the intrusion into his passion, he asked. "Who are you?"

"My name, sir, is Aloysius Waechter."

"Ah, you represent the Sheik." Alex ran his tongue over his fangs willing them back.

"Yes, sir,"

"Do I owe my freedom to you?"

"For now, we still have some work ahead of us."

"Very well Aloysius, you'll take a flight back to New York City. I'm going to take my wife on an express flight."

"Sir, I must take this opportunity to remind you that you have not been cleared only released temporarily. I am expected to assure your presence at all legal proceedings."

"Noted and thank you, but no one will ever know that I've left the country. I will be traveling as Alexander and using no human method of transport. Whenever you need me, I'll be there."

Alex grabbed Lina and tapped a rift. He landed in their apartment in Macedo Tower. Kissing her with a firm yet compassionate embrace, he inhaled her scent before releasing her. "I've so missed you, woman."

"Show me how much, Papi." Lina cooed.

"That'll have to wait." Alex's voice was stern. "Where are my sons?"

Lina's eyes grew wide, "Archimedes is with Mirella and Jesus… and I left Max with Jack and Miguel. Why do you ask,

Amor?"

Alex watched as Lina headed to the bedroom, he was a few steps behind her.

The look of cold, calculating viciousness transformed from Mirella's face to one of happiness. Her little face with its blackened eyes and sharp fanged smile was a picture of certain, pending death a few moments before.

Alex sighed, thankful that he could see Archimedes in her arms safe and sound. Taking a moment to digest that his newest son was safe, he took a deep breath acknowledging that his eldest son was in the hands of a vicious killer.

"If Archimedes is here then it has to be Max."

Lina shook her head, "Jack and Miguel wouldn't leave him. They know how vulnerable he is right now."

Alex walked towards Lina, "Mirella we'll be back. Please watch over Archimedes until we return." He grabbed her hand and looked upwards before he moved them to Max's penthouse suite.

"Max?" Alex called.

Jack and Miguel rushed out of Max's office.

Alex didn't let go of Lina's hand to receive the embrace from Jack or Miguel. "Where's Max?" he asked with hope written over his face.

"We left him in South America." Jack hung her head.

"South America?" Alex looked at Lina who shrugged her

shoulders then back at Miguel and Jack.

"A quick debrief is in order," Miguel offered.

Alex pursed his lips and moved to the sofa pulling Lina with him.

"I gathered some information from Florida when you last saw me. I brought the information back to Max and we dissected it. Pieces of info were missing, so Max sorted through Louis' memories, to find the soucouyant that delivered the package from Chen."

"I was attacked by two Chinese vamps in lockup sent by Chen."

"Well, a long story short," Miguel paused, "This Chen is not Chen, but the offspring of Ying Zheng, commonly known as Qin Shi Huang."

Alex gritted his teeth. "The original?"

"Yes, I believe so. Max was determined to defend your honor. He promised that he would return to the Tower after we left the Amazon. The last thing he said was for us to go ahead and he would be moments behind after cleaning up a few loose ends with Joey."

"Joey?"

"A male witch from the Amazon?"

"Ah," Alex nodded, remembering the name. "Is there anything else?"

"I think you need to talk to Leonidas and Ishtyn," Lina

offered.

"Why? What's up?"

"I think that I have meddled in vampire affairs too long, my love." Lina smiled.

"Fair enough, I'll see them in time." Alex sighed.

A crackling in the air made him jump off the couch. He snapped his wings open and dropped a full four inches of fang. He was ready for battle.

"Joey!" You should find a way to knock. You almost got eaten."

"Not likely, old man," Joey laughed.

"I'm glad you're here," Alex grinned closing his wings, walking over to the witch, and embracing him. "We have a problem, and I need your help."

"Max?"

"Yes."

"I was getting negative feelings, which is why I came unannounced." Joey shook his head. "I told him it was a lousy idea to go to China. But he was determined to prove that he was your son through and through."

Alex hung his head. "He should know by now that he'll always be my first born."

"I don't think this is about title," Joey smiled.

"I don't think so either," Alex's smile was not a hearty one. He remembered what it felt like to be his father's son.

The plumes of dust rose like the clouds from a volcanic eruption. The dust was stifling, and visibility had become difficult with each prancing hoof. He was a magnificent steed, though his ears were flattened back with flared nostrils and wide eyes. Fear seemed evident. But what was creating such a fear? Was he not familiar with his handler, Philoneicus? Alex recalled. He blinked as his memories continued.

King Philip II had become enraged that neither he, nor, Philoneicus could tame the stallion. The beast had excellent lines with an amazing stamina. His coat dazzled in the sun. His nose had felt like the softest velvet.

You can't ride that beast. You're not old enough. He'll kill you. Have you no wits at all boy? His father's ranting had fueled his pride. The beast of a stallion, with his broad head, arched his powerful neck before rearing up each time he saw his shadow long before him. Could it be that the horse's weakness was the sight of his shadow? Alex smiled. *As a man, mounting Bucephalus required much strength and agility. As a child of twelve, a boost was needed, though he was smart enough to point the horse in the sun's light, so his shadow was behind him.*

"Look, thee, out a kingdom equal to and worthy of thyself, for Macedonia is too little for thee."

The immortal words of King Philip II, his father, played on repeat in Alex's head. He knew that they were not the words of a proud father, but rather, of a shamed man. For his father never believed him to be of his flesh. Time never softened the edges of honesty; it was a cruel, sharp emotion. Alex knew the reason why he had labeled himself the Son of Zeus was due to the need to be accepted as someone's son.

Alex sighed, "I'm coming for you, son, just hold on."

CHAPTER TWENTY-ONE

"Are you alright?" Chen twirled Max's retainer between his thumb and forefinger. "So young and yet you have the determination of a king." Chen spun around to face Max, "Are you a young king?"

A burning ache throbbed at each of Max's wrists. The room was dark and his head fuzzy. As far as he could remember, he lay naked on a mechanical table shaped like a cross. The bolts that pierced his hands to keep him pinned to the table no longer hurt. A metal collar retained his throat and ankles. The burning came from the thin lines surgically cut from wrist to elbow that Chen was keeping open with silver clasps doused with magic. His vampiric blood ebbed in a steady stream collected by the table. What they would do with his blood, he didn't know. His head lolled aching for peace. "What do you want?"

"I should ask that question of you, as you entered my country without permission."

"I came only to speak with you," Max's tongue was thick in his mouth, "and ask you to cease this vendetta against my family."

"You are young and don't understand the value of honor." Chen spun. "Besides, you will live and be allowed to return home eventually. Do you not like how I've chosen to keep you alive?"

Max closed his eyes; the horror of his actions flooding his memories and weighing on his soul.

"No!" Max yelled, as he saw Chen make a familiar motion with his hands.

He rolled his eyes hearing a small pitter patter of feet. A small girl stood in front of Chen trembling. Max whispered trying to shake his neck, "no, no, no." Some part of him knew that she wouldn't hear him. Chen's lips moved, but his words were only intended for her.

Tears of blood welled up in his eyes spilling on to his cheeks before hitting the table. She walked towards him. She looked so young. Her black hair was straight and parted into two ponytails perched high upon the crest of her head like a school girl. Her pale alabaster skin was perfect and unblemished. She was beautiful. She wore a white button down shirt tied at her midriff and a tartan mini-skirt. Her rose aureole pressed against thin cotton shirt; they shone through demanding attention. Her lips were a rosy pink, her bottom lip much fuller than her top lip. He begged her in his head to go home when she opened her mouth to receive his flaccid penis.

He screamed in anger, dropping his head onto the table afraid of the history that would repeat itself. He felt her climb on top of him, crawling towards his face.

"Please stay away," he begged.

"Mr. Max," she whispered just as all the others before had whispered, like they were reading from a script. "I do not make you happy, Mr. Max?"

"Go away," Max pleaded.

"I'm afraid, Mr. Max," she whispered still moving towards him.

"Go home," Max could feel his incisors lengthening and the change in his eyes as the room became brighter and she became no more than prey.

****

"That never gets old," Chen laughed motioning to a low-level vamp standing at the door. "I have to see my father, make sure this one stays alive. He has strong blood. Keep sending in those tramps every hour to sustain him."

"Yes, boss."

"And should we get any visitors, leave him. I want the blood transported to the safe house."

"Yes, boss."

"Fail me and you will die the most painful death after I pull your teeth. Am I clear?"

"Yes, boss."

Chen growled, taking in the pile of young Asian girls discarded like a pile of trash at the side of the blood collection table. "And clean this up while you're at it."

CHAPTER TWENTY-TWO

"Alexander, are you alright?" Miguel asked.

Alex blinked, Miguel's voice making an impression on his mind. He turned slowly to see that concern had displaced the usual stony-faced façade. "I'm..." he swallowed, "I'm okay, just worried about Max."

"We're worried about him, too." Jack started.

"We did ask him not to go. We asked him to exercise caution."

"I can't believe he lied to us and went anyway." Jack pulled on her lower lip.

"Lied? How did the exchange go?" Alex asked.

"He said he had some loose ends to tie up and he'd be along right afterwards." Jack muttered.

"Ah, in his mind he might have had a different perspective. After all, if he showed up right now would his statement still hold truth?"

"I suppose," Jack mumbled, "you're defending him."

"To a point." Alex sighed, "I know what it's like to have people tell you all the time that you cannot or should not do something when you know full well that it is within your capability."

"Like father like son," Joey smiled. "Perhaps I can help?"

"How so?" Alex queried.

"Well, I'm no Max, but I'm not so shabby with a computer. Plus I'm a witch, so I can try and locate him."

"Have a go at it Joey and keep me informed."

"You're leaving?"

Alex looked at Lina. She was worried. He took her in his arms. "I've missed you so much."

"I've missed you too," she breathed.

Alex heard the huskiness in her voice and his body responded, "I never imagined that a self-inflicted stay in lockup would be so traumatizing; separated from my family and friends, causing all kinds of havoc on your lives let alone mine. It leaves me to wonder whether it was all worth it." Alex threw his hands up at the luxurious penthouse that surrounded them. "Is it truly all worth it? I could have begun again, or just found somewhere to settle with you and Archimedes. Max is a grown man. He needs to make decisions for himself."

"Amor," Lina smiled, "while you may have decided to save your empire, we all stood beside you or behind you. This is our way of life too. I can't speak for everyone, but I like how we live. No one entity should be able to push us over the edge."

"Okay, then you should know that I'm going to see the original Ying Zheng."

"There's no point in me coming then," Lina laughed.

"Agreed, besides we already have one son missing, I would much rather that you are close by. Not that I don't trust Mirella or Jesus, just that I know that nothing will happen if you are here."

"I will be here waiting for your return, my love." Lina smiled.

"You are so beautiful," Alex smiled.

"Now you are just talking like a freshly sprung man," Lina teased.

The levity worked wonders on the stress that was tying a knot between Alex's shoulders.

"Oh and Amor?"

"Hmmm."

"You might want to avoid Aloysius; he's in your office." Lina cautioned.

"Okay my love, and babe?"

"Yes."

"If someone comes after anyone while I'm gone, please don't hold back. Let's save as many innocents as we can; I want my enemy crushed."

"Agreed, Amor," Lina nodded.

"I'll be heading down to the armory before I leave." Alex gave his wife a longing gaze then snapped his wings open. He gave them a good stretch before wrapping them around his body transporting him to the armory. Finding his feet on solid ground, he snapped his wings closed. He ran his fingertips over the rough stone walls until he came to the end. Finding the stone he needed, he pushed it until the wall popped out enough for him to slide it manually backwards, straining with his vampiric strength until the door was retracted. He stood in front of a metal door.

"Activate access panel."

"Welcome Alexander, your voice has been confirmed," the automated voice responded by producing the requested panel.

He laid his hand in the palm shape and curled his lip as a mechanical spike pierced through his hand.

"Identity confirmed. Access granted."

The metal door slid backwards grating against the stone particulate caught in the tracks.

Alex walked in. "Close all access to the armory." He walked towards his weapon collection and picked up a samurai sword with an ivory handle. Intricate carvings were etched into the ivory and all along the blade itself.

He nodded, satisfied with his selection. Moving onto some

protective gear, Alex smiled as his helmet with three plumes caught his attention. "Not today." Instead, he selected his favorite dragon skinned full length trench and matching pants. Changing quickly, he grabbed the sword sliding it into the hidden sheath and snapped his wings open.

"Voice command." Alex took a deep breath.

"Exit Alexander." He found himself back in the hallway; a quick look over his shoulder told him the armory had sealed itself. Nothing was visible to the naked eye. Pausing, he flexed his wings and tapped a rift that opened in mid-air. Alex flexed his wings to catch an updraft and landed on the railing of the mountainside chateau. He would have called it an ancient imperial palace. It stuck out of the side of the mountain, but there weren't many houses, let alone anything this majestic on the mountain.

Every layer of the house had a different purpose and was connected by stairs that appeared to go on for miles. It seemed only right that the very king that sponsored the concept for the Great Wall of China had an equally formidable home.

"Oh what do we have here?"

Alex didn't turn around; he was an ancient vampire in what many would consider the most ancient part of China. He remained perched on the railing.

"You are American, right?"

Alex inhaled the Chinese vamp's scent and wondered if this

was Chen, the offspring of the mighty Ying Zheng. He hoped not. If it was, it seemed like the apple fell off the cliff a million miles from the original tree. This vampire, old though not ancient, had no honor.

Movement on the stairway half-way up the mountain's side caught Alex's attention. Flowing robes seemed to float as they ascended the stairway to the Monastery on the neighboring ridge.

Alex flexed his wings and caught the air. He loved the feeling of flying, although he rarely had the opportunity to do it for pleasure.

He landed on the stairs snapping his wings closed and began his ascent by walking the last remaining thirty stairs.

By the time he was five stairs from the top of the staircase he was confronted by the man he supposed to be Chen. Alex inhaled again hoping for a scent of Max; either the vamp washed with pungent soap to rid himself of the scent, or he didn't do much of his own dirty work. All he would need was a bite. The blood would tell him exactly who the vamp was and what he had done, if anything, with Max.

Alex continued to walk up the stairs ignoring the goading. In the old ways, the ancient vampires would disregard all they believed were insignificant.

"America, don't you know who I am?" Chen goaded. "I will destroy you."

Alex smiled. Fighting words. Now he could give the little parasite some attention, a mere exhibition of his power that would cause him some pain, not kill him. If he were indeed Zheng's son, a dead son was an insult - even a deadbeat son.

Alex stuck his hand out, his palm faced outward as if signifying stop. Chen went flying backwards, stopped by the retaining wall of the stairway. His head leaned over the wall as Alex closed his fingers.

"Zibeing!"

Alex turned at the sound of the nick name that only Qin Shi Huang would use. It was an old term that showed respect for someone considered virtuous. That was the trait that had won the ancient king over. Alex grabbed the hilt of the sword and grunted, releasing his grip on Chen who crumbled into a ball at the base of the wall.

Alex moved towards Qin Shi Huang, no further words were exchanged. He removed his shoes as he entered the house of worship and also removed his sword, which he placed in front of him before sitting cross legged. He stared at Qin Shi Huang in silence.

Two sounds broke the silence, the noise of Chen scuffling to awareness outside and the noise of a young woman shuffling in with tea.

Qin Shi Huang nodded to Alex, who returned the motion before lifting his cup to his lips and drawing in some of the warm brew.

"It has been a long time, Zibeing."

"So it has, Ying. So it has." Alex smiled at him. "How does time treat you?"

"It is a misnomer that time is on our side. Change is not kind to the ancient who cannot embrace the new concepts that life now offers."

"I share the same sentiments." Alex returned his cup to the rectangle saucer and waited until The King started the conversation again.

"You have done well for yourself."

"I am a warrior, as are you. Our kind is extinct. I have been forced to adapt to survive, but I still value honor as the old traditions demand. I teach my son to do the same." Alex reached for his cup.

"A son, Zibeing?"

"I have two." Alex wanted to laugh. The feeling came over him like he should break out some photos. Who would have envisioned two old kings sitting around talking about children over tea like a couple of old grannies? Maintaining his serious façade, he buried his lips in the warmth of the tea.

"The sword looks as good as the day I gave it to you."

Alex fingered the hilt, "I take exceptional care of it. It remains a valued friend, like you." Alex lowered his head in a bow.

"After so many years, you have come, why?"

"My family has been dishonored." Alex replayed the events and added, "I have come to ask for my son. I offer…" Alex touched the hilt of his sword lowering his head.

Ying Zheng grunted as he got to his feet. Alex didn't move, except to turn his head when Chen came to lean at the opening of the house of worship.

"Father, why do you disgrace us by talking to that American?" he clutched at his neck.

Ying Zheng was silent. He walked out to the balcony. Alex couldn't hear what he was saying to his blood heir. He saw the ancient vampire sink his fangs into the neck of his son only to remove them seconds later. He wiped his mouth in disgust.

It took Ying Zheng a while to return to the door way of the house of worship. "Zibeing, come."

Alex grabbed his sword and sheathed it. "Ying?" He saw blood tears flowing down his face. Chen was squirming on the floor, slowly regenerating.

"Please tell me?" Alex couldn't wait for Chinese protocol and hoped he hadn't offended The King.

"Zibeing, my family owes you much. I don't know if your son is alive. I have witnessed some horrors at the hand of my son. I have become an old man to think that I could trust him."

"Where is he Ying Zheng." Alex shook him, "I must try and save my son."

"The Fujian province, in Xiamen," Qin Shi Huang smiled,

"I'll give you twenty four hours to get your son. Make sure that you are not in China after that."

Alex nodded.

CHAPTER TWENTY-THREE

"I found his phone?" Joey exclaimed.

"Where?" Miguel jumped up from the couch and walked into Max's office. Joey was trying to command and direct six panels.

"I have it—here!" Joey hammered at the keys until the satellite dish responded, displaying the street in Xiamen.

Miguel scanned the screens and dematerialized. He materialized on the side street and scanned it.

"Yes!" Finding the phone was a small elation. He picked it up, the battery was dying. Max's home-grown app was spinning on the screen. A limo pulled out slowly from the garage in front of him. Miguel shoved the phone in his back pocket and reached for the hilt of the sword which lay between his shoulder blades in the form of a tattoo. Unsheathing it, a white brilliance surrounded him.

"Alexander, I think I've found Max. Where are you?" Miguel thought as he mustered his energy and sprung upwards.

"Closer to God than you for a moment."

"Why is that?"

"I was visiting an old friend. Now where are you, so I can hone in on your essence?"

"I'm in Xiamen."

"That's where the old king directed me.

"Awesome, I have Max's phone. I think he's in a building nearby."

Miguel landed on a roof. He hacked off the lock of a nearby door and scurried down the steps. "Alexander where are you?"

"I'm here."

Miguel grabbed Alex's forearm, "I'm glad you could make it."

"Wouldn't miss it for the world."

Miguel and Alex fought side by side; Dark and Light Warriors, fighting for a common cause, honor and the freedom of one fledgling vampire. The Chinese vampires fell one by one, as sword and talon decapitated the heads of some and extracted the hearts of others.

"I'm following my nose here." Miguel mumbled, as he walked

down a hallway with his sword at the ready. They turned into a dimly lit room.

"Is that Max?"

"Sure looks like it," Miguel responded.

"Oh shit." Alex held his stomach.

"What kind of contraption is this?" Miguel asked, looking at the table.

"Ancient Chinese secret," Alex muttered touching the table. He yelled, touching Max's restraints and stepped over the bodies of girls. "Miguel, I can't get him out of this thing. I can't touch it. The bindings of his wounds have magic or something and the table itself seems to be rigged."

Miguel pinched the top clips embedded in Max's skin pulling them free. "The clips smell like witchcraft. The curse seems to only affect the undead. Max is still alive, he's regenerating." Miguel smiled, "it's slow, but he's still with us."

He pinched the tops of the metal studs forcing them down until Max's limbs were freed. With sheer angelic strength, he broke about the restraining collars. The anklet by Max's left foot gave him some trouble springing back unexpectedly and biting him on the finger. He placed the victimized digit in his mouth.

Max woke up gnashing his teeth fighting for his life.

"Easy, son," Alex called.

"Dad?"

"I'm right here."

Alex watched as Max flopped back onto the table.

"Take him Miguel, please. Take him home."

Miguel nodded.

"Give him some peace."

****

Alex nodded as Miguel dematerialized with Max in his arms. He looked around the room tracing the path of the blood collection. Not finding any tell-tale signs disclosing where the blood had gone, Alex set to work lining up the dead girls so he could decapitate them. He didn't want to take any chances that they could be reanimated—they had suffered enough.

His cell phone rang as he got to the last head. He made a swift cut before reaching into his pocket to extracted it.

"Hello? Leonidas is that you? —Hey old friend what's up? —Nope not doing much right now I have a moment to chat? Where are you?"—In the UK? I'll be right there. I have to talk to Ishtyn anyway."

Alex closed the phone and blew on the palm of his hand igniting a flame. It ate all the bodies in the room.

He transported himself to the next floor in another attempt to trace the blood collection. Spying what looked like a false column that could be hiding conduit, he moved between floors quickly until he reached the third floor. Everything stopped. The conduit was exposed and a single droplet of blood hung suspended in the air. It had coagulated and was frozen in time.

"What are you up to?" Alex asked as he scanned the room. It was sterile and uncluttered. While collecting blood did not seem to be a foreign concept, the collection and subsequent transportation of vampire blood did seem odd.

The room held nothing unusual in it. The walls were barren as was the floor. The only thing out of place was the missing piece that should have sat below the hoses that stuck out from the conduit like a Medusa coiffure.

"I'll find out," Alex muttered before tapping a rift to London.

"Old friend," Alex smiled embracing Leonidas. "What's up? We didn't get a chance to catch up in Florida given the circumstances."

"I know Alexander, and it is those circumstances I want to discuss with you."

Alex looked at the warm invitation from his friend to take a seat on the park bench. They were meeting out in the open where they could easily make an assessment of who was watching and listening. So many times being out in the open was safer than being in a private enclosure.

"Your wife recommended I talk to you," Leonidas smiled, "she is quite a woman."

"Did she now?" Alex leaned back into the bench sprawling his legs. "And yes she is."

"I've been struggling with some of the decisions that I've

made which may have placed you at a disadvantage."

Alex sat up before leaning forward on the bench. He clasped his hands. "Speak."

"A few years back, I got lonely. I invited a woman to my bed. She took advantage of me and not in the typical fashion. I was induced into a sleep where she raided information. Bits and pieces. I allowed myself to be stupid. I believed that I cared for this female only to find out that I had been lured by a trickster. Perhaps I had become a lonely old man, but the ramifications are all the same no matter how you look at it." Leonidas sighed. "To satisfy myself, I have endangered not only you, but the entire vampire community."

"Where is the disadvantage part? Men have fallen victim to women year after year after year. In my mind, this is not any different." Alex shook his head. "The burden on your shoulders was weighed more than you should have had to bear. The fragility of our process is the fault of the Vampire Council and not yours. We have not changed with the times and there lies the root of the problem."

"I found out that Ishtyn made some unscrupulous decisions, and that has placed you at a disadvantage, too.

Alex opened his mouth to speak, but shut it seeing Leonidas' hand up suggesting that all questions wait until the end.

"How did that impact you? I needed to protect my own hide first. Even today, I was more concerned about the actual job of getting back on track."

"What made you want to come clean?"

"It was something your wife said, and now I just want to say, thank you and goodbye."

"Leo, we're immortal, we are bound to run into each other sometime." Alex sat up and stopped fiddling with his hands. "What did you do now?"

"I told the Vampire Council. I told them of my actions and they insisted that they expire me." Leonidas sighed, "It's for the best I suppose."

"I see you're at peace with it." Alex shook his head. "Guilt has consumed you my friend. Although, I must say, my perspective is a little different."

"You're not even angry that I didn't warn you of the situation."

"Some part of me is saddened to think that our friendship did not carry enough weight for you to consider confiding in me. However, as you became engrossed in covering your tracks and trying to save everyone from the slip, I'm seeing it that you had the larger purpose in sight, instead of a singular friend. That makes it okay for me. It's not like you sat back and did nothing and let me walk into an ambush."

Leonidas hung his head.

Alex could see a smile of relief creep into his old friend's face, "Go in peace, old friend."

Alejandro?

My Love?

Where are you?

London. Is everything alright?

You have a visitor, will you be returning soon?

Who is it?

Ishtyn of Cairne.

Detain him by whatever means possible, I'll be right there.

Alex closed his mental link with Lina and patted Leonidas on the leg. "I have to go." Alex watched Leonidas nod, "Don't go running off into the sunlight yet. Better days are in store."

He heard Leonidas' laugh echo, as he snapped his wings open and tapped a rift back to Macedo Tower in New York City.

As he walked out of the rift, his dark, leathery wings hovered above him. Ishtyn of Cairne and his signature flaming red hair stood in his living room. Not knowing what had transpired, disgust and contempt rose in this stomach like bile from a heartburn party.

He reached out to him, burying his talons in the ancient vampire's shoulder and held him in a vice grip, sealing his cocoon with his wings. Alex dropped his fangs sinking them deep into the ancient flesh without regard for any pain. The blood memories hit Alex like a runaway freight train. "You have betrayed us!"

Still holding onto him, Alex tapped time's rift and landed in the center of Stonehenge.

"No, please." Ishtyn fell to his knees.

Alex backed away from him until he was flush against the rock. A fire lit above his head.

"The calling…" Ishtyn whispered. "It's started." He crawled on his knees toward Alex who glared at him.

Alex watched him whirl around as another ancient vampire arrived hooded. He moved back into position against the rock and a fire lit above the hooded vampire. Alex didn't take his eyes off Ishtyn. The flaming red hair became matted as the old vampire fretted in the dirt stirring up the silt. He whirled with the arrival of each ancient vampire. He could feel the drain of the sun as it began the new day initiating its climb across the sky. He moved his lips speaking vampiric tongue. Extending his arms, he reached out on either side of him to share the memories he had gleaned from Ishtyn. Electric magic arced between each of his hands and the next vampires hands until the circle was formed. Not even the crackle of the magic could suppress the wailing Ishtyn was making. He was worse than a hysterical banshee.

When the sharing of memories was complete, Alex dropped his arms. The blue sparking ceased, and the fires extinguished.

The time had come for the decision. As Alex initiated the calling, he would be the last to decide. If the ancients agreed with him, they would verbalize their decision and leave. If they disagreed, they would remain and the remaining would be responsible for Ishtyn's actions for the rest of his life. He would have no influence over anyone or anything. Alex rolled his eyes over each ancient vampire as they made their decision and disappeared. He was the last vampire looking at Ishtyn, now stripped of title and lineage.

He rose, stretching his hand out to Alex in a final plea.

CHAPTER TWENTY-FOUR

"Look at what the cat dragged in." Lucifer sat on a crate staring at his talons. He was in human form, wearing a Versace tone on tone suit. He nodded to the demon at the warehouse door to allow Chen to pass.

"I have something of interest to you." Chen smiled.

"No swagger today? No America? No glib remarks?" Lucifer smiled.

Chen looked at his feet shuffling them from side to side.

Lucifer jumped off the crate and dusted his hands. He walked around Chen, examining him closely. "You looked like you were just stitched up." His skin looked like it had just regenerated and was still quite raw in places. "After you were peeled like an apple."

"Can we get on with this?" Chen mumbled.

In the single beat of a hummingbird's wing, Lucifer was beside Chen with his fangs grazing his ear, "Make no mistake my once cocky little vampire, you exist because I allow it and no more." Lucifer inhaled. "You think your lineage gives you an edge? I'm guessing you just had your expectations reset. No worries little bug. I can help you get to the top."

Lucifer watched the light return to Chen's eyes. He was pleased the little bastard showed him respect by averting his eyes every time he circled.

"Who did the number on you?"

"My father, Qin Shi Huang." Chen muttered.

"Ooh," Lucifer laughed, "ain't no whooping until daddy dearest lays it down."

Chen kept his head bent and shuffled his feet.

"What was it over? The ass whooping I mean."

"He claims I brought dishonor to a vampire named Alexander."

The smile faded from Lucifer's face. He bit into Chen's neck savoring the bitter sweetness and filtering through his memories. "You'd better be careful when you go up against Alexander. For now, stay away from him." Lucifer spat Chen's blood on the floor.

"Yes, sir."

Lucifer wiped his mouth on the Chen's sleeve raising the vamp's arm to do so. He noticed the briefcase that the vampire was clutching.

"By the way, you need to intake more B12. What did you bring me?"

"I want to renegotiate our contract." Chen stood up clutching the briefcase in one hand and holding his neck in the other.

"Are you in a position to barter?" Lucifer cocked his head, allowing his natural yellow demon eyes to read Chen.

"I have maintained our first contract bringing you vast quantities of blood in exchange for power. But I need to be stronger and more powerful."

"Is that so, show me what you've brought and then we'll talk about whether or not we'll make an amendment to your contract." Lucifer extended his arm, motioning Chen towards the rear of the warehouse to an area surrounded by crates that were stacked almost to the ceiling. Behind them, two chocolate brown suede couches flanked a glass table, whose legs were fashioned from gigantic horns. "Have a seat."

Chen obliged, laying his briefcase on the glass table. He undid the latches. Lucifer raised an eyebrow when he hesitated for a moment before raising the lid. He leaned forward. The briefcase held four vials. "Talk to me. What do we have here?"

Chen reached for a vial containing black powder. "This was made from very powerful blood." He sprinkled a granule onto

Lucifer's palm.

Lucifer called a demon, "Four human women." He pulled his handkerchief from the inside pocket of his suit and laid the silk square on the glass table. The grain of black powder looked quite out of place.

"These other two vials are different grades from the first, but my leverage and negotiating power comes from the fourth." Chen grinned picking up the vial.

Lucifer regarded it with suspicion. The vial contained a dark crimson liquid. "Let me see it." He reached for the vial. It was larger than the others, and the blood hadn't been processed to a powder form. "It's just blood." He started to hand it back.

"Shake it." Chen nodded.

Lucifer shook the vial. A sparkle caught his attention. He rolled it slowly to balance the level of blood to get a look at the substance that glittered like a diamond from within the blood. "Is that...?"

Chen grinned, "We believe that to be angel's blood. I gave some to a human and the results were spectacular. The human thought they were invincible and flew off the top of a sixteen story building."

Lucifer handed the vial back to Chen, remembering the amount of angel's blood he had shed with his own sword. Angel's blood and their dust had wildly addictive qualities for humans. "So you propose to produce a drug with the blood of vampires and angels?"

"Not just one drug. Two drugs. The vampire blend gives them a high like a longer lasting version of ecstasy, while the angel blood makes them successful and empowered."

"That sounds very good," Lucifer smiled, "like you are doing the world a great service."

"Well, there are some side effects to not staying on them and long termed use, but that's not my problem." Chen smiled.

"How do you plan on getting more of the angel blood?" Lucifer asked his curiosity at its peak.

"I'm told there's an angel in New York on a regular basis."

"I told you to stay away from Alexander."

"I had planned to follow your direction expressly." Chen bowed.

"Let me think on it." Lucifer smiled, "I'll call you."

CHAPTER TWENTY-FIVE

"It seems that I have you to thank," Leonidas laughed looking around as he held the cell phone to his ear. London was full of people out and about enjoying the cooler night air. To fit in, he pulled his jacket closer and tightened his scarf. He usually held a dislike for mingling with people during the winter months; they were difficult times for vampires to blend. Humans usually got rosy cheeks or red noses when the cold hit their faces, vampires did not. Humans would create a warm mist when they exhaled in the cold, vampires could not without help.

"And what would you be thanking me for?" Alex asked.

"Oh, I don't know Alexander. Living another day, seeing

another moon rise, or for getting me out of that solitary life." Leonidas smiled throwing his hand into the air.

"You sound quite cheerful and full of life, Leo. I haven't heard you so in many years."

"I think that I became tired of the solitary life eons ago. With the council so set in its way, there didn't seem to be a way out." Leonidas stuffed his hand in his pocket and trudged through the oncoming crowd of people. "So, thank you again."

"I'm not the only one that makes decisions on the Vampire Council you know."

"I know, but I'm sure my name had already been discarded."

"So you have all of Europe now?"

"So I'm told, any tips?"

"Find Rebecca."

"Who is she?"

"She is the blood line heir named by Ishtyn. He bound her also."

"Why a second?"

"There's a price to pay when you ask for magic to be performed on yourself. You either pay with something from you or someone else. In this case, he paid with Rebecca; I guess he felt she was his to give away because she was the blood heir."

"Where is she now?"

"Your guess is as good as mine."

"So how will I find her?"

"As an ancient vampire with territory, you will encounter many situations where you either can't follow the money or the trail, or just something. I would recommend that you find yourself a good witch. Become familiar with your territory. Find out what works and what doesn't, and visit your Master Vampires so that they truly pledge their allegiance to you and not just because they are bound. They could break the binding if they wanted to; you want them to want to stay."

"A witch, huh?"

"I'll send a witch to you, and after he helps you find Rebecca, he'll help you to find a good, good witch."

"Alexander?"

"Hmmm?"

"I'm in your debt," Leonidas stopped, realizing the seriousness of his statement.

"I think that's two, now."

"So it is, thank you." Leonidas tapped the touchscreen to end the call and sighed. To owe Alex a favor once, was one thing, but twice in one lifetime was overwhelming. He shoved the phone into his pocket and began walking again, a piece of paper folded into a square rolled into his view catching his attention. He bent down and picked it up stopping to unfold it. The paper was plain, white, and ordinary, like the kind found in printers all over the world. Each fold was precise. No one piece overlapped the other and the creases held no pulls, as it would have if a finger rubbed it into position.

Join me for a cup of tea at Maggie's.

Leonidas looked around. He spied an Irish corner restaurant named Maggie's and crossed the street. Horns blared from the little speeding cars as he crossed the road looking the wrong way before he set out. *Damn British. Driving on the opposite side of the road.* Leonidas could have kicked himself for forgetting to look. It was something he would have to learn, being out of the States.

A bell rang as he pushed open the door.

A jovial waitress greeted him with an unmistakable Irish lilt, "Hi love, it's getting cold, isn't it."

"Yes, it is," Leonidas smiled.

"Go on ahead then, dearie, he's waiting for you in the back room there," she smiled.

Leonidas nodded, loving the natural rouge in her cheeks. The coloring in her face was from laughter rather than the weather. A trait he would have loved to have in his first life or his afterlife. He walked in the direction where she pointed. Worn carpet made a path through the yellow wallpapered room littered with pictures. Unsteady tables littered in a makeshift order. He ducked to fit through the doorway and smiled seeing only one person sitting in the café.

"Hello, I'm Leonidas." He extended his hand.

"You should never shake a witch's hand that you don't know," Joey answered smiling. "You can call me Joey. Alexander sent me, so I know a little bit about your request."

"Joey?" Leonidas loosened his jacket.

"Yes, were you expecting something like Esmeralda, Gertrude, or Winifred?"

Leonidas laugh was filled with apprehension. His mind recollected few fond memories involving witches. He exhaled trying to maintain a sense of calm. "What's in a name? Let's just say, I wasn't expecting Joey."

"Fair enough." Joey smiled.

"I thought witches were female."

"Are all nurses female?" Joey smiled.

"Well no, but then what are Wizards?"

"Wizards are like the Doctors of Magic and witches are like nurses." Joey laughed.

"So are they women wizards then?"

"No, they are called Sorceresses."

"So how do we get started?" Leonidas asked shaking his head.

"What can I get you both?"

Leonidas looked up at the rosy cheeked waitress and opened his mouth to speak, closing it when he felt the pressure of Joey's hand on top of his.

"A pot of tea would be nice, Earl Grey with no milk, and sugar on the side, please. Thanks love," Joey smiled.

"Earl Grey?" Leonidas scratched his head.

"The loose leaf tea has oil of bergamot and lavender in it.

Great for warding off evil spirits. So I'll make a protection spell before we locate our missing lady. You might want to ask her to borrow her smart phone."

"I have one?" Leonidas reached into his pocket and placed his phone on the table.

"Is that a US phone?"

"Yes."

"Man, you are going to get hit with some serious roaming charges if I use it."

"It's okay, I'll manage. Go ahead and use it. I saw her phone sticking out of her pocket. It's an old flip phone. I doubt it even has a screen on it." Leonidas laughed.

The tea was placed on the table with smiles and nods. He watched the waitress round the corner and nodded to Joey when then were alone.

Joey poured himself a cup of tea, "Do you want any?"

"No, thanks."

Leonidas followed his movements as he set the teapot back on the table, flipped the lip open, and used a fork to fish out the tea leaves giving them a firm squeeze. He arranged them around the rim of the plate setting the phone in the center.

Joey held his hands at a forty-five degree angle and began chanting under his breath.

"I'll not be having the craft done in my establishment," the waitress ran in waving her hands.

Leonidas blackened his eyes and dropped his voice, "Go and make some tea."

"That'll not be working on me vampire."

Leonidas could see her trembling as she fought his persuasion, "We are trying to help someone who is lost. Give us five minutes. You are protected from any evil." He gave her a genuine smile and nod. As she walked away, he could hear her mumbling about putting up a new sign for folks like them.

Joey held his talisman over the cell phone screen that he had set to Google maps and closed his eyes. Leonidas followed the talisman as it swung within the protective circle. The screen went dark, "Do you need me to unlock it?"

He stared at Joey. No response.

The screen finally lit back up and the talisman stopped swinging, though still suspended from Joey's hand. His eyes were closed. Leonidas peered at the phone when the maps stopped moving.

"Ireland."

"There's a large church in Southern Ireland. It stands in ruins. Beneath the grounds lies a hidden chamber. I saw her chained to the gates.

"Aye, that's an Abbey."

Leonidas pursed his lips, "How much do we owe you? I'm guessing you're Maggie?"

"Aye, I'm Maggie. And that'll be two pounds twenty." She

held her hand out shaking her head. "I don't normally cater to the likes of you two, but there's something about ye that feels right. You be careful when you go out there. It's a thin place. There are things worse than the lot of you out there."

Leonidas smiled, pushing a ten pound note into her hand, "Thank you, Maggie, we appreciate the warning."

Joey handed Leonidas his cell phone and they stepped outside.

"So, Joey are you coming with me?"

"Yes, sir, Alex asked me to help you with Rebecca and help you to find the witch. I've helped you with the witch; I just need to complete the second part of my obligation."

"You've helped me with the witch?"

"Hmmm, Maggie." Joey smiled, "You two seemed to have hit it off. It'll be up to you to make the introductions and formal request."

Leonidas smiled, "Very well, and Rebecca?"

"I need to make some preparations. Be ready to meet me there at midnight."

Leonidas headed back to the hotel and lay on the bed. He turned on the television leaning forward hearing the news flash.

"A mysterious figure of sand and ashes has been erected at Stonehenge. Officials are looking into the vandalism, while scientists are trying to understand the significance. The wind is a little headstrong here this evening, but if you follow the camera, you can see the statue made of ashes has been protected by the outer circle of stones. The history of Stonehenge has been estimated to be a giant clock or calculator. The appearance of the statue has awakened many myths. One of which claims the circle to be a ring of execution for the Children of the Night. Whatever your beliefs, no one can answer who this is a statue of and how it got there. Wait—we have a local farmer who claims that he saw lights in the circle last night but didn't go to check. Let's see if we can cut live to the farmer..."

The news reporter's voice faded as Leonidas focused on Ishtyn. He turned off the television and transported himself to Stonehenge. Keeping his distance, he walked around the frenzy until he found an angle out of the wind. He walked in a straight line toward the man dressed in a white hazardous materials suit, who was standing in front of Ishtyn's remains.

Leonidas lowered his voice, "Look at me." He channeled his voice to the man. His head turned slowly.

"Touch the statue," Leonidas blackened his eyes and channeled his voice.

Blood welled in the man's right nostril before breaking into a bubble. The sound of the bubble bursting and the sight of the blood splattering inside the suit made the man flinch. His right hand flew upwards, hitting the remains of Ishtyn. The ashes caught the winds which roared over the plains, hungry to consume all in its path. Uproars of horror echoed around the circle.

The man took off his helmet and marched over to Leonidas who normalized his eyes.

"What's your name?"

"What?" Leonidas gave his attempt at an English accent.

"You made me do that?"

"Are you off your rocker? I'm all the way 'ere and you there. Can't blame me because you hit the blimming thing." Leonidas started mumbling under his breath and walked away almost bumping into Alex.

"Rusty?"

"Maybe," Leonidas grinned giving Alex an embrace.

"I spoke with Joey; he said you guys are heading to Ireland."

"Yeah, we found her."

"You'll need my seal authorizing you to travel in my lands." Alex smiled.

"Seal?" Leonidas looked puzzled, but took Alex's ring from him anyway.

"Yeah, you have Europe which doesn't include the UK. As we meet in London, I have quite a bit of traffic when the Council is in session, so there's always a lift. In the past, I have always granted Ishtyn free pass into Ireland because he was born there. I just want to cover my bases with you so the Celts don't skin you, pin you, and leave you for dawn."

Leonidas pushed the ring onto his finger feeling a wave of

magic rush over him. "What was that?"

"Protection. When you are done, give it to Maggie," Alex laughed. "I have to run; I have some amends to make."

"I know that smile. Thank you, friend, I hope to repay the debts soon." Leonidas grinned as he teleported himself to Ireland.

The mists were coming in from the sea. They rolled and swirled across the ground like groping fingers. They devoured every tree and savored the graves.

Leonidas shivered, not from the cold, because vampires relish the cooler temperatures, rather the mists were causing his skin to prickle. Joey was right, this was a thin place. A mystical place, where the worlds were separated by an exceedingly thin veil of fabric and cross-over was evident.

He placed his hand on the wrought iron gate that guarded the cemetery. Purplish electricity crackled over his hand absorbed by the seal of Alexander. Leonidas smiled, thankful that Alex had thought ahead; then again that was Alex. In two millennia, he was always either one step ahead of the game, on par, but never behind.

"Wait."

Leonidas turned to find the shadowy figure of Joey walking up the hill at a good pace. The mist swirled about his feet as if disturbed by his every movement.

"You have Alexander's seal, good thinking," Joey smiled.

"You smile a lot for a witch," Leonidas chuckled.

"What? Should a witch look miserable?" Joey smiled again. "Besides, you laugh a lot for a vampire."

"That's because I haven't been around people for so long that it's refreshing."

"How can you avoid people? They are everywhere as soon as you walk out the door."

"Well, that's just it, isn't it," Leonidas laughed, "who said I ever left or walked out the door?" he pushed open the gate which creaked until it was shut again.

"Don't step on any graves," Joey cautioned, "I would skirt the outside of the cemetery by the wall until we get to the Abbey itself."

"I see a side door, or do you think we should go to the front."

"I don't know if the front door is an option."

"You're right," Leonidas smiled, "For us to take the front door now would mean that we would have to cross the graves. Don't you think that the chambers would be towards the rear of the church anyway? I'm just thinking about how others are laid out."

"I'm not a real church goer," Joey grimaced.

"No worries, I'm not judging. I think we'll be just fine."

They skirted the perimeter of the graveyard. Reaching the doorway of the Abbey was of little celebration; they still had to find Rebecca. The interior of the Abbey was enveloped in blackness that consumed the remains of the ruins.

"I think I hear something coming from below." Leonidas whispered. He turned his head to see Joey's nod. Plunging forward into the depths, he could imagine the abbey in its glory. The knave lined with pews and soft light filtering through the stained glass in the deepest pitch of the night; he sighed, side stepping a pile of crumbled rocks. Walking to the rear of the ruins, he looked up to see the mists coming through the open windows, like wraiths creeping down the side of the walls.

"We need to hurry."

Leonidas heard urgency in Joey's voice. There was something unnatural about the way the mists were creeping in. The wailing from below got louder. Leonidas grabbed Joey's arm, "I know you don't like to hold hands, but time is off the essence." He used his preternatural speed and headed straight for the source of the noise.

He stopped short in front of a blonde haired woman chained to a wrought iron gate under the Abbey. She appeared limp with her weight suspended from her wrists. Her head hung forward, her blonde hair looked like strands of silver silk in the darkness. She was dressed in a white nightgown. Her skin was also pale, giving her an ethereal appearance.

"Are you okay?" Leonidas reached out to touch her.

Her head whipped upwards with a glaring wild stare, "Don't touch me. Don't touch the chains. Don't touch anything I touch." Her voice was near guttural.

Leonidas moved backwards in surprise. Her head fell forward again. "What do you think Joey? Can we help her?"

"Help me. Help me, please help me," Rebecca pleaded, as she strained against the chains.

Joey held his hands over the chains. "She's in there somewhere, but she has been restrained by old magic. If you free her by touching her, you will take her place. If you kill her when both she and you touch the weapon at the same time, you will stand in her place."

"Kill me!" Rebecca swung her head to stare at Leonidas. Strange enough, he felt like he was actually looking at the real her.

"What happened to you Rebecca?" he asked.

"I have been bound to a devil. I am a god fearing woman."

"You are a vampire." Leonidas corrected.

"I do the work of God." Rebecca glared at him. "No matter what form my shell has."

"I see your dilemma," Leonidas grimaced looking around. "Joey, can you move this gate?"

"Move it where?"

"Move it out of Ireland and place it on the beach in the land with bright sun."

"I can."

"Without touching it?"

"Most definitely without touching it."

"What are the ramifications?"

"I'm not sure yet," Joey walked up to the gate. "I think this gate serves a purpose. I believe that it is the physical barrier before the crossing beyond the veil."

Leonidas peered into the darkness in the tunnel beyond the gate. As a vampire, the dark didn't bother him, he had perfect vision as did any child of the night; but the darkness in the tunnel was different. This darkness was impenetrable.

"I see nothing."

"You won't see beyond the veil." Joey sighed. "I don't think we can move her until we figure out how to break the curse, the hold, or how to…"

Leonidas walked back down the hallway remembering the rebar he had seen laying on the floor from recent vandalism. Pulling the rebar out of the concrete, he picked up a rock and began smashing it against rebar until it became flat. He took the flat metal and sharpened it using the rock. Sparks flew until the metal edge shimmered.

"I could have summoned a sword," Joey laughed.

"And what would the result of magic against magic been?"

"I don't know, but you have a point. What are you going to do?"

"I'm going to take her head."

Rebecca lifted her head curling her lips back to bare her

fangs. She hissed like a big cat. Her eyes blackened as her survival instinct kicked in. "I will kill you."

Leonidas ignored the incessant threats spewing from Rebecca's mouth. To him, she was a lost cause. She had died the day she allowed herself to be chained to the Iron Gate. He stopped fashioning the blade and looked at her, "How old are you?"

Insults and threats flew. Leonidas lowered his voice using vampiric tongue, "Rebecca be still."

When she stopped moving, he continued, "How old are you, Rebecca?"

"I have five hundred years."

"Someone has been feeding her." Leonidas dropped the blade placing it on the floor in front of her. "Either you know magic yourself, or you are being fed. Which is it?"

Maniacal laughter filled the cavern and the chains around her wrist unraveled like a rattlesnake warding off his prey.

"Just as I thought," Leonidas smiled. "You're like a possessed soul."

Once free from her chains, Rebecca moved towards Leonidas. "I had no intention of killing a vampire and a witch tonight, but there can be an exception I suppose. I can make and break my own rules."

"You have no power except whatever magic you can wield. You may have Ishtyn's blood line, but you do not have his territory."

"That matters not."

"No?" Leonidas cocked his head, "That means you don't even have Ireland. The magic in this land belongs to the Master that governs it. Surely you have felt the change?"

Rebecca's eyes grew wide.

Leonidas continued to push her. "Little by little, I'm sure you've felt the land receding from you. Alexander is the Master of these lands."

"Noo, these were Ishtyn's lands."

"Is that what he told you, Love? He lied to you," Leonidas laughed, "he had naught more than a free pass."

"Still, they are not your lands," Rebecca spat.

"That may be true," Leonidas waggled his hand hosting Alexander's ring. "But I hold the Master's seal; the land will grant me safe passage."

A shrieking wail pierced the air from Rebecca as she lunged. Leonidas picked up his crude blade and thrust it towards her. He watched it lodged in her chest. She stumbled backwards. He was sure to let go before it reached her, hoping that he had used enough force to have it pierce her black heart. He watched her falter.

"Joey, I want you to call upon the strength of this land to protect its own. Tell them that this is not the Rebecca that would have cared for the land; rather a broken entity that has been possessed by a powerful demon who will drain the land of all it hosts and any magic that lingers."

Leonidas watched the life light back up in Rebecca's eyes as she attempted to pull the sharp blade from her chest.

Joey rocked as he chanted; extending his arms, he implored the highest spirits before dropping to his knees - never breaking his rhythm.

The mists rolled in with speed groping the walls. They raced towards Rebecca. Leonidas took a step closer to Joey, feeling a little safer next to the chanting witch. The mists swirled around Rebecca's feet as if they were feeling, or sniffing like a curious dog. When Joey's chanting increased in tempo the mists got angrier, climbing her staggering body, threading like ropes around her torso arms and neck. The mist took on the forms of faceless wraiths that grabbed the makeshift blade and plunged it deeper into her heart. One wraith pulled it out only to pass it to another who cut off her arm provoking screams from Rebecca. Leonidas took a step backwards as the scenario repeated itself over and over until nothing was left of Rebecca but a pile of ash. Joey stopped chanting and fell, placing his hands on the floor to steady himself. Leonidas reached for him. He halted when Joey raised his hand in warning. By the time he looked up, the mists receded without a trace.

"All magic, Rebecca, has a price. I'm sorry it was you." Leonidas sighed, "C'mon Joey let's get you some sustenance."

CHAPTER TWENTY-SIX

Alexander sat behind his desk twirling a pencil. His inbox overflowed with business emails to catch up on, and yet he sighed, choosing to stare in contemplation at the child snuggled up on his chest. The brown soft curls framed his little head. He looked like a cherub. Alex smiled knowing better.

Although an infant, Archimedes had quite a temper. Little razor sharp talons appeared at the ends of his tiny fingers as he clawed the air when in a tantrum. His fangs hadn't come in yet, but the instinct to latch on like a tenacious pit bull was already in place.

His mind drifted to the last stop he had made.

The melodramatic palm trees shook in frenzy as the breezes toyed with their fronds. The ocean's cleansing salt carried on the air throughout South Florida. He stood leaning against the light post by the edge of the sidewalk watching the tourists navigate South Beach. He had closed his eyes as her scent reached his nostrils. His eyes picked her out through the throng of the crowd. She was wearing a white long sleeved shirt with matching fitted running shorts. Her hair shone in copper glory under the glow of the sodium lighting. Their eyes locked as she ran. She had felt the connection, he was sure.

The feeling was confirmed when she stopped short in front of him. He eyed her long lean legs drawn upwards by the silver swirls on her running attired landing on her green eyes.

"Do I know you?" she had asked.

"Amelia, I would hope that I made a lasting impression." Her scent was enthralling.

"You look decidedly familiar. How do you know my name?"

"Our interlude was quite memorable, I could never forget. Did you destroy the video as I requested?"

The milky white of her skin betrayed a blue pulsating vein just beneath the surface. It became more evident as she scanned her environment for invisible ears.

"I don't know who you are, or how you are privy to a private conversation, but you should go and make sure you never cross my path again."

"I cannot make that promise. I plan for our paths to cross again, soon."

She had parted her lips in silent objection and yet she had taken his hand when he offered it to her, pulling her into the secluded terrace of a restaurant. The trees surrounding the terrace offered a quiet retreat from the bustle of South Beach. Alex smiled, his powers of persuasion were much stronger when he was not focused on imaging Lex.

She sat without hesitation next to him on the bench drawn by more than his suggestion. Her eyes wide with questions remained locked in his without persuasion. Her hair was soft and silky.

"Amelia O'Hara, I have to ask you again. Did you destroy the video as I asked you?"

Her voice was breathless with anticipation and her pupils dilated with unbridled desire. And yet she hesitated. "I did."

"But?"

"The New York Detective, Edward Trattoria had already reviewed the video."

"Why?"

"He told an officer he wanted to keep an eye on Lex Macedo. One of my officers had allowed him to see it before its destruction."

"I need to make you mine."

"I want you, too."

"You don't understand yet, but you will. I will take care of you and your desires soon enough." Her blood was sweet. He had allowed himself to bury his fangs deep and indulge himself with her essence. To a passerby, they would appear like overzealous lovers. Her head had arched back cradled against his one hand, his head buried in her neck in the kiss of a vampire. Her arms embraced him with a lover's caress. Her skin felt smooth and a *little salty from her sweaty run when he licked the wounds to seal them. He had bit his thumb and rubbed his blood on her lips. Her tongue licked his blood and her eyes opened in recognition of the taste. In the same instance, he imprinted his seal on the nape of her neck with the remaining blood on his thumb.*

"Alexander?"

"Amelia?"

"I belong to you?"

"Yes."

"What does that mean?"

"Continue your routine, I will visit you in the days to come and I'll explain. Right now, you should finish your run and go home." He had rested his forehead against hers sending her a mental image of them locked in a passionate kiss. Her lips parted to receive his, but he placed the actual tender kiss on her forehead.

The obtrusive ringing of his phone broke his recollection. "Hello, Macedo here."

"Alexander, this is Aloysius Waechter."

"What can I do for you, Mr. Waechter?"

"We have thrown enough doubt into the mix that the various agencies have taken the case under review both internal and external. A pre-trial hearing will be set several months from now to finalize whether we'll move forward with charges and a trial. Some discussion is also being had as to whether or not the trial will take place on US soil."

"Why is that?"

"Well, the companies in question are not US companies; which is why the discussions have taken a turn, but Lex Macedo is considered a US person."

"Good job Mr. Waechter. Keep me informed." Alex smiled, as he closed the connection. He picked up his ring absently; it having just appeared on his desk. "Thank you Leonidas." He slipped the ring back on his finger.

"How are you guys doing?" Lina smiled walking into the apartment.

"We're doing fine, he fell asleep on me." Alex smiled. "Is he down for the day?"

Lina checked her watch swinging it around to see the face, "Yes, sunrise is almost upon us. He won't be up until night fall."

Alex passed Archimedes over to Lina watching her bottom move beneath her dress as she took him to his crib. He caught his lower lip with his teeth. A low growl escaped his lips with the onset of desire. From the self-denied torture of being in jail, to his recent encounter with Amelia O'Hara, the want for Lina was almost uncontrollable. He watched her hips sashay as she walked.

Supernatural speed took him to the door of his bedroom. He closed it behind him waiting for her to finish putting the baby down. His chest heaved. His eyes roved over her body from her slender ankles to her firm and muscular thighs, up her taut abdomen to her large breasts.

"Lina," Alex knew his voice was husky and laden with lust.

"Amor," Lina walked into his arms.

He bent his head to nuzzle in the scent by her neck. It was euphoric, a mixture of death that drove him crazy. He sank his fangs into her neck drawing moans of pleasure from her. His talons ripped through the matte jersey dress that she was wearing to cup her round bottom. He moved forward with a slow purposeful step, savoring each moment that it took him to get to their king sized bed.

He reached to cup her other butt cheek, and felt Lina's arms wrap around his neck as she in turn sank her fangs into him. She lifted her legs and wrapped them around him as he walked her over to the bed. She relinquished her hold on him and he withdrew his fangs from her neck to rain kisses down her body as he lowered her to the bed. "You are so beautiful, my love."

"You are biased, Amor."

"That may be true, but you are still beautiful." Alex smiled, looking into her perfect brown eyes. Her curly black hair fanned out on the bed like the snow angel. "I love you."

He looked into her eyes, wiping blood tears that threatened, "Why are you crying?"

"Because," Lina shook her head, "I'm not sure that I've heard you say it often. I've felt it, but to hear you say it feels…"

Alex cut her off with a kiss. There was no rush, she was

his forever; an immortal that would share eternity with him. He made love to her; pouring every passion and emotion into their union. He needed her to know, feel, and understand exactly what she meant to him.

****

Lina pulled the covers to her chin, smiling as she snuggled up on Alex's chest. She ran her fingers lightly over his muscles enjoying the coolness of his skin. The doorbell rang; she looked up into Alex's titanium grey eyes. "You expecting anyone?"

"No, but I'll check it out."

He got out of the bed. Lina couldn't help but smile at her husband's lean torso. His muscles rippled as he balanced to pull on his Armani slacks. His six-pack muscled abdomen clenched when he looked down to button the pants and buckle the belt before pulling on the zipper.

She snuggled deeper into the sheets, fully sated, listening with intent as he padded to the front door leaving the bedroom door cracked. Lina jumped at the sound of the familiar voice that greeted Alex.

"Hello?"

"My name is Lane."

"Ah, the Black Wolf."

"You've heard of me then?"

"Indeed, you'll be wanting to speak with Lina?"

"I do, but you have me at a disadvantage, sir. I don't know your name."

"My name is Alexander."

"You're a vampire."

"I am."

"You are her mate?"

"I am her husband."

"I see," Lane paused. "If you don't mind, I would like to request the return of the Red Wolf's skin."

"That, friend, is business that you must conduct with my wife. Wait here. I'm sure she'll be just a moment."

Lina slipped out of bed. She pulled on a pair of jeans conveniently hanging out of the hamper and grabbed one of Alex's shirts to put on. She managed to paste a smile on her face meeting Alex at the bedroom door. "I heard the conversation." She stuffed her hands in the jeans back pocket noting that her palms were sweaty. Was she nervous?

"Okay, my love, I'm going to go to the roof top."

"Is everything okay?" Lina searched his face. She knew that Alex was extremely possessive and in a quiet way uncomfortable with being jealous."

"Yes, I just want to watch the sun come up," Alex smiled, "and this is your business. I don't want to seem like I'm involved in your affairs."

"Nothing happened you know." Lina smiled, feeling a little

uncomfortable. "I mean, we just shared blood, I'm sure you know that already."

"I blocked the memories," Alex smiled, "I just wanted to love you right now, not see what you've been up to in my absence."

"Oh." Lina thought back to their lovemaking realizing that she hadn't felt the onslaught of memories; she had just enjoyed their union. "Okay Amor, I just want you to know that I wouldn't jeopardize what we have."

"You're fine, honey. Handle your affairs. I trust you."

Lina smiled into Alex's eyes. She felt the warmth in his voice. Thoughts of Ishtyn and his blood heir being bound to her bombarded her. "Thank you my love, but I know you don't like heights. Don't feel like you have to go out there just for me."

"While that's true, I'm comfortable with the top of Macedo Tower."

Lina stared into his eyes as he placed his hands on either shoulder, "Okay, Amor, I meant everything I said."

Alex laughed, "I know that I've been uncomfortable with him and your past; I also meant what I said and most of all, I do trust you. I know you wouldn't get involved with vampire business just like I'm making a point to stay out of your wolf business. The rest of the underworld we'll tackle together."

Lina smiled, wondering just how far she would have stayed out of the vampire business if push had come to shove. Clearing her throat as Alex disappeared, she walked into the living room.

CHAPTER TWENTY-SEVEN

"Hey there, what are you doing up here?" Miguel sauntered towards Alex.

"Hey, brother, how are you?"

Miguel smiled accepting the embrace from Alex. "You look like you were interrupted?"

"Not quite, just giving Lina space to deal with the Black Wolf and the Red Wolf skin dress."

"The Black Wolf is here?"

"He is."

"I thought that he is, or was a sore subject for you?"

"You know Mig, I have never been on the other side of the fence. As a king, I paraded through countries and commanded.

People bowed to me. I conquered many for little reason other than to have it. I've had men and women lining up to feel the invasion of my prick and you know what else? Men have had my back for two reasons alone: fear and greed. And now, I find that I need to trust and depend on others to do what they would want to do based on a single, yet complex emotion called love and I'm rather astounded."

"You were quite the warrior then," Miguel laughed, thinking about how that sounded and wondering whether he should recant and revisit the statement, "that didn't come out as intended."

"No, but I know what you mean," Alex laughed. "Either way the self-induced stint of incarceration did what it was supposed to in drawing out my enemy. It also gave me plenty of time for reflection. I find it strange that the people who have my back are absent, and over two millennia later, others do so out of love. This is a stronger position than any command. Am I so thick that it took so long?"

"Opportunity, my friend, doesn't always present itself at a convenient time." Miguel laughed, thinking of his own love with Jack and just how long he had existed before he met her and, or, frail mortality.

"True enough, brother," Alex laughed, "And so I came to the rooftop to think and watch the sunrise."

"Suicide?" Miguel raised an eyebrow.

Alex laughed, "Back in the day, I remember when I could walk in the sun with no issues. Now, through the depletion of the ozone layer and increased ultraviolet light, it's true, I have sensitivity to it; I'm too old my friend to perish from sunlight. It would be a painful existence, not enough to make me perish. Only the fledglings would ash right away."

"Like Max?"

"How is my son doing?"

"He's suffering from more mental trauma than anything else."

"Were you able to wash him with peace?"

"I did, but his trauma is self-inflicted; the worst kind. He is beating himself up over the quantity of women killed at his fangs."

"Hopefully he won't lose himself from it. It'll either kill him or it'll make him stronger."

"That's harsh, Alexander." Miguel thought about the truth of the matter and couldn't agree more with Alex's assessment.

"Yes, it is Mig and as unfortunate as the whole thing was, it's still a true statement. He needs to find a way to get over it and make whatever weakness into a strength." Alex sighed.

"You know he is in love with Samantha."

"I do."

"Have you been to see him?"

"I have. I will allow him one more day to wallow in the mud of his existence before I go to snap him out of it. I would prefer that he pull out of it himself. He needs to find strength. He is my first born son and nothing will be easy for him. While I don't want him to lose his human edge, if I make things easy for him should there ever be a time where he needs to step up, he will suffer a worse fate. This love of his should help to bring him out of it, not push him deeper into a hole."

"As much as I don't want to agree, I do." Miguel smiled.

Alex sighed, "This is my favorite part of the sunrise. I love the way the rays of light span out like fingers clawing through the darkness, reclaiming this side of the world for a moment."

"It does feel like a majestic moment. I have watched the break of dawn with similar feelings after war."

"I have a bad feeling my friend that the war has not yet begun. Have you given a thought to what the Chinese were doing with that blood?"

"I have, and haven't had any positive thoughts." Miguel stared at Alex. "I haven't been able to trace their location."

"Yet another reason I want Max up and running. While I don't advocate revenge, he will have a stock in seeing this through."

"You think he'll know?"

"I think he'll have the best idea of us all. He may have heard things either in his conscious or subconscious. He is the only one who has been with Chen." Alex shrugged, "It's worth a try."

Miguel nodded, wondering if the young vampire would be up to the challenge.

"Well, let me go and see Max. I haven't caught him awake yet."

Miguel decided that for all his talk, Alex looked a little dejected, "He might be sleeping again, I washed a wave of peacefulness over him before I left." He nodded at Alex, grasping his forearm before watching him disappear.

*****

He leaned against the support arm of an antenna watching the crescendo of the sun. A black bobbing dot on the horizon caught his attention. It seemed to be flying towards him. The closer it got, the figure seemed to take on another shape. Miguel stood shielding his eyes from the sun as it took its position in the sky. He couldn't quite make out if the figure coming towards him was the silhouette of a bird. *But check out that wingspan. That would be an extremely large bird.*

Deciding the bird was of no consequence, Miguel turned. Walking over to one of the air-conditioning units, he jumped up on the unit to take a seat when large claws pierced his shoulders pinning his arms to his side. A cold burst of something wet landed on his face. His vision began to tunnel. Images of dark wings and black feathers filled his mind. Bright sunrises with flashing red lights on tall poles that reached for the heavens dominated his brain. He blinked. A slow grating feeling seared across his eyeballs until the images plagued him no more.

EPILOGUE

"Oh, yea honey, work it, work it, work it," Lucifer sang as he watched a pretty young thing manipulate her body around the pole. He threw back another shot of vodka, neat. It was smooth like her skin. He rested his free hand on the curly tresses of the other, whose head was bobbing between his legs. "Oh yea! Take it Mamita Linda."

The saucy music quickened his libido. He sank deeper into the microfiber chair at the Gentleman's club.

"Oh, Luke, you're amazing," the young woman hopped off the stage and plopped herself on the couch next to Lucifer.

"Yea baby, you have no idea, go dance for Daddy again," Lucifer slapped her on her bare rump drawing giggles from her.

He patted down his pockets hearing his cell phone. "This better be good."

"I have the Angel."

Lucifer stared at the screen on his blackberry. "I thought I told you to stay away from Alexander."

"I did not disobey your direction. The opportunity was seized when Alexander was not present."

"Really?"

"Do we have a deal?"

"Bring me some manufactured product and then we'll talk. You still have to prove whether or not you can mass produce the stuff. Harvesting the source will be a challenge, as will be maintaining your grasp on it."

"This is not an issue, I assure you."

"Your assurances aren't worth your pot or your piss. Put your money where your mouth is and bring me the manufactured product. Once I see it then we'll talk." Lucifer looked at the screen before ending the call and returning his focus to shaking naked flesh before his eyes, "C'mon honey, you have Daddy's attention now. Take it from the top. "

About the Author

Bitten Twice is an author who primarily writes in the paranormal romance and urban fantasy genres. She released the first in the Macedo Ink vampire series in October of 2010.

Bitten Twice currently lives in Hollywood, FL with her family. Courageously in love with one man and two children, together they care for the family's two dogs. Bitten is a lifetime member of the Florida Writer's Association and an associate member of International Thriller Writers.

You can follow Bitten on the web:

Facebook: BittenTwice

Twitter: @bitten2ice

The Web: http://www.bitten2ice.com